PARLEY IN PASSION

I0525641

by

CHARLES NUETZEL

WRITING AS "JOHN DAVIDSON"

The Borgo Press
An Imprint of Wildside Press

MMVII

SECOND EDITION

CONTENTS

INTRODUCTION

This is another one of those looks behind the scenes, an expose of the film making industry as seen through the eyes of a fella putting words to paper. As noted elsewhere, especially in my *Hollywood Mysteries*, it can be a tough town on those struggling young actors and even for the big named stars.

In this book I take a man I named Joe Dickerson and run him through the paces of the film-land survival course, a jungle of woman begging for parts and willing to do what is necessary to get them. And I added a super star who is Big Time Trouble for the studio. You're standard mix of players, including the lovely young actress desperately attempting to get her first break in films.

I don't know, but these kinds of complex little jaunts into the California sunset have always fascinated me. Having lived in Southern Cal all my adult life (and since I was 8 years old) has given me some sense of the landscape, the scene, so to speak, and a feel as to how things truly are. I've even worked in the business as a young man. All of which makes the settings rather comfortable and intriguing. I have been here a number of times in real life and in fictional creations of my own making.

This story, perhaps, takes a closer look at the passions involved and the hungers that drive people to take one another out on romantic interludes and even develop a few meaningful relationships.

Ah, the wonder of romance! We all seek it; and the Industry feeds on our longing for love and our need for fascinating people and places.

So, why not offer up another rendering of the ol' tune

of love and passion and intrigue—Hollywood style?

> *It looked as if Joe Dickenson was going to make it in the film-land jungle. But there were nasty roadblocks. Mainly: he had to bring Carole Clement into line for the studio. Then there was the problem of tearing lovely, sweet Ann, whom he had fallen in love with, from the clutches of the lustful Mari— and he knew it would take a master of emotions to pull it off...*

Enjoy the sin of it all!

—CHARLES NUETZEL
Thousand Oaks, California
July 2006

CHAPTER ONE

Joe Dickenson had seen a lot of beautiful women in his time—it was his business seeing beautiful women. They flocked to Hollywood like hungry she-wolves, and they were willing to do just about anything to get the attentions of men like himself.

She was tall, well proportioned, high-breasted, and blonde, dressed in a green sheath that accented every curve and line of her body. Her name, Ann Farrow.

She was standing by the window, looking out at the mountain scenery surrounding them.

"It's a lovely place, Joe," she murmured in a lilting voice, looking at him for a moment. "I hardly expected this...last night, when you suggested we go off someplace."

"It seemed a little more interesting than the Canton party," Joe grinned, finding it impossible to keep his eyes off her thrusting breasts. The low cut neckline revealed that their shape was natural, not puffed out by falsies.

Ann Farrow turned, stared at him, leaning against the window, her hips thrust outward, as if challenging, her bosom high pointed, taunting, inviting.

Even the long ride to Big Bear Lake, which had followed a long night a-boozing, hadn't drained his natural instincts to take that body and love the hell out of it.

So far they hadn't touched each other since leaving the party.

But memory of that hot kiss on the patio of the large Beverly Hills home still burned fiery in his mind.

They had been introduced by Mari Thornton, a young starlet who had been around long enough to know the right people well enough to get a few minor parts in pictures. Joe

7

and Mari had been through the bed routine a couple of years back. Mari was a tall red-head, big boned, high cheeked, large full lips, but slightly cool. But Mari gave out to enough men to get her way around Hollywood.

Joe had been standing in the study, next to the bar, sipping scotch and water when Mari came up with Ann.

"High, love," Mari greeted, throwing her arms around his neck, pressing her hips close, cushioning her breasts against his right arm as she planted an open mouthed kiss on his lips. It was a standard greeting for Mari.

"Hi, kid." Joe patted Mari's fanny, smiled, his eyes already taking in the woman standing just to the right of her. What he saw burned an immediate fire. "Who is your friend?"

"I thought you'd like her," Mari announced with mock jealousy in her deep voice. "This is my new roommate, Ann Farrow."

"Let me know more," Joe said, nodding at Ann.

"I have other fish to fry," Mari told him, patting his cheek. "Take it up with Annie!"

With that Mari exited.

For a moment Joe stood there looking at Ann, saying nothing. She had deep green eyes that returned his gaze evenly.

"I take it, Ann, that Mari told you all about me!" Joe offered, knowingly.

"Some," Ann countered. "Fix me a drink?"

She stepped up close to him, leaning an elbow on the bar. Her head topped at his nose and she held his gaze with her eyes, wide, innocent of any message, yet seemingly exploring.

"What'll it be?" Joe had already made up his mind to take her to Big Bear—if he could. And there was little doubt in his mind; Mari never had a roommate who wasn't willing to be very cooperative with men.

"Scotch?"

"Fine."

He reached for the Scotch bottle and his right arm brushed her breasts. The feeling was exciting, soft, supple.

"Where's Mari been keeping you?" He handed over a

stiff drink.

"Hasn't! Just pulled in with her a week ago. A friend of mine from home arranged things."

Her face was still upturned, her eyes still gazing deeply into his.

All he had to do was bend down to kiss her lips.

"And home is?"

"Carmel. Mari needed a roommate and I needed a place to drop my body from time to time. And, well, Mari's helping me some in making connections."

"Trying to break show business?"

"Isn't everybody...*here!*" She tipped the glass to her lips, tasted, then after hesitating a moment took a swallow.

"And Mari said I might be of some help? Is that it?" he suggested, looking down her neckline. The sight sent a shiver of desire through him. He was tempted to explore with his hands, to feel the warm flesh, to know the bite of a hardening nipple.

"Yes, she said something like that," was the answer, very soft, low, even warmly sensual. It was obvious that the woman was totally aware of what he was finding so difficult to ignore. She smiled, a bit amused, a bit teasing, a bit flirtatiously at him.

"And?" he managed, huskily.

"Well, what does it take to get ahead in this town?" she inquired.

"Right connections. Plenty of experience—"

"At acting, I hope you mean," she almost laughed at that.

"Why of course. What else?"

"Well, the way you're ogling my … dimensions, so to speak, I somehow get the impression that acting talent, agents, credits, whatever, have little to do with what you guys are really after."

"Shame on you. That makes us sound—"

"Like you're a normal male on the make, I suppose." Then hesitating only a moment she added: "Are you?"

"What?"

"Oh, on the make," she offered with amusement flashing in her lovely eyes.

9

"How the hell did you turn things around?" he inquired, a bit dazed. She was charming, smart, witty and lovely. Very sexy.

"I'm a woman. You're a man, and men just never get to outclass a smart lady."

"Oh?" now it was his turn to be amused.

"Well, we never let you know the truth, of course. We're just helpless little dumb things with boobs hanging out to catch your eyes, and we just don't know what you make such a fuss about. And then you take advantage of us pure, innocent little girls." She pouted. "Is that about right?"

"God! You're really something!"

"That's illusive."

"Well, hardly."

"A compliment?" she wondered.

"More…like a reality check! I'm stunned."

She merely smiled at that, her eyes lowered, moving away.

Neither of them spoke for a while. But his whole attention was literally feasting on her, eyes flowing all over her lovely body, her neck, hips, eyes, nose, breasts, legs, lips. Moving madly from point to point, wanting to touch her, hold her, kiss her, literally devour her from head to foot.

He felt dizzy, light headed.

The liquor was finally getting to him. And this woman was power-driving him to a wild state of raw desire. He simply wanted to get away, take her somewhere to be alone together. Escape from everything else that was happening to him.

He'd been at the party for a couple of hours already, boozing it too much, trying to forget the problem of Carol Clements. The day had been a long one, and he had sweated out the difficulties of a leading star being late for work. The situation held up production and was getting him personally in hot water, since it had been his idea to hire the skidding "CC." Carol had done okay in films until the last couple of years, then she'd started sliding. Being a problem. She was boozing too much, sleeping out with too many men and being a general hell on set—topping off her antics by *not* appearing on time. She couldn't get a job with any other studio.

10

Because of her personal difficulties of being a good investment for a studio, it had been possible for *Bennick Studios* to get her cheap to star in *Roaring Guns.* Joe was mainly a casting director with big ideas of getting into the production end.

Walter Bennick, studio boss, had trimmed him down good that afternoon because of Carol Clements not showing up on the set on time. Joe had talked to Carol, and she'd promised that this was the last time, that she was terribly sorry.

Then there was his wife who wouldn't leave him alone. Rather, his ex-wife. But that was another story; he didn't want to think about that, either.

So booze was one way out- one way to escape the problems of his personal and professional life.

He focused on the woman standing in front of him. She was staring directly at him, now and she smiled warmly, and as their eyes met once again, said: "Mari told me you had some important position at the studio ... but...everybody here seems to have important positions."

"So true." He laughed, touching her shoulder, mainly to see what her reaction might be.

She merely stood there, not moving.

It was as if those moments, a short time before, that swift conversation, had never taken place. They were suddenly aware of one another as total strangers.

Yet he knew what he wanted to do. He wanted to know every part of her body, from head to foot. He desperately wanted to sweep her off her feet and carry her out of the party and into some private place where they could get to know one another in a totally intimate way. If that were possible. And chances were, it would be very much possible.

"You're a bloody attractive woman."

"Thank you. And...Mari didn't do you justice!"

"Oh?"

She smiled, revealing even white, gleaming teeth. "Said you were tall, dark and handsome."

"And what's wrong with that?"

"Didn't say you were...well, attractive." She edged closer, but there was still far too much distance between them to suit him. There was promise in her eyes as she continued to look up at him. Then for a moment they stood there frozen.

The spell broke and Ann stepped back.

"I do have to mix, Mr. Dickenson." She turned, as if to leave. "Business, you know."

"Maybe you won't find anything helpful out there...any more helpful than is right here, Ann." He offered, before it was too late.

"Oh?" Ann turned, surprised interest showing in her features.

"Well, with all modesty aside, I am in a position to help a girl of your apparent abilities."

"What abilities do I have?" she mocked him.

"Afraid I don't know, outside of a very attractive body. A good looking woman can go far in Hollywood, if she knows the right people."

She was slowly moving closer. "And you might help me?"

"I'd damned well like to help you, Ann."

"I think I'd like that," she told him, this time standing so close that her breasts just touched his chest. "I think I'd like that a lot."

They talked some after that, between drinks. A little later they went into the ballroom where a small combo was playing and several couples were dancing.

Later, out in the patio, the garden surrounding them, the moon high, bright, casting highlights over her face, Joe pulled her close to him, very close, thrilling to the nearness of her body, exciting to the lushness of her.

Their lips met, open, moist. And as he probed deep into her mouth with his tongue she strained tightly against him, her lips captured his kiss as if thirsty beyond control.

"Let's get out of here," he offered after they had broken away from each other, catching their breaths.

"You making a proposition, Joe?" she murmured throatily.

"Call it what you like!"

"Okay, I think it would be nice." With that she took his arm and let him lead the way out of the large house of their host, the studio boss, Walter Bennick.

12

They had driven all during the early morning hours and by the time they got to Big Bear Lake the sun topped the mountains. Before driving to his cabin they had stopped off for a large breakfast and then he had gone to a liquor store to get Scotch.

Now, standing in the bedroom of the three-room cabin, looking at her, Joe felt the normal excitement of a man about to discover the intimate secrets of some Goddess. The build-up had been tremendous.

"It's a nice bed," Ann observed, stepping over to the large double bed, touching it with fingertips. She was leaning over, looking at him, her neckline deep, full, revealing creamy white flesh.

"Want a drink?" he offered, suddenly nervous.

The palms of his hands were sweaty; a hardness constricted his throat.

"Not really."

She sat, pulling her legs up under her. It was an inviting pose, wanton. A lock of blonde hair fell over her forehead and she brushed it aside.

Joe moved to the bed, as if drawn by some steel wire. He slipped down beside her, slid an arm around her waist.

Ann didn't move, didn't lean closer. For a long time she sat there, supported by her right arm, looking at him, teasingly.

"It's awfully late...or, early...to be making love," she told him, a twinkle in her green eyes.

"What difference does that make?"

"That depends on the man," she challenged him.

"And you wonder if I'm the right kind of man?"

"That's a secret I'll keep to myself!" Still she didn't lean closer. It was as if she were playing some kind of cat and mouse game with him.

"I'm tired...terribly tired, Joe. It was a long drive and..." She yawned lightly.

Almost angrily, because he didn't know for sure if she were serious or not, Joe yanked her to him, his left hand covered her breast, his lips crushed to hers.

Her mouth was open under his and he felt the heaving of her breasts against his exploring hand.

13

It was like diving into a deep pool, being surrounded suddenly, gasping for breath, but not wanting any air.

Her lips found his, cushioned, fitted, her right hand caressed the back of his neck, then he felt the tangle of her fingers as they gripped his hair, pulling.

Somehow his hand had slipped under her dress and found soft warm flesh.

Joe knew from that moment that he had found a real special woman in Ann Farrow. The passion throbbed through her blood like fire, her body was a lava flow of heat, desiring, wanting to smother its victim.

"Love me good, Joe," she murmured, pulling away from the embrace, lifting slightly to unzip her dress. She found his hands and worked them under the top of her dress, which had fallen away from her shoulders. "Love good, Joe. I like my men to be good. Real good." She mouthed his nose, touching it with the tip of her tongue, then caressed her lips down to his as he explored the fullness of her breasts, worked the dress down to her hips.

They locked on the bed, lingered in the lover's embrace before continuing on into the caresses that would make them both naked.

There was nothing coarse or common, nothing cheap or dirty. This was a matching of two healthy animals, both taking the other, equally seducing.

And her body was even more beautiful naked. The breasts were supple, self-supporting, the nipples pink and well formed, eager to excite to a man's kiss or caress. Her stomach was smooth, creamy, flat, warm. Her legs firm, and lithe. Her movements flowing, a perfect match to his own passionate actions.

When they finally had tired of the playful build-up, their bodies became one gasping unit that fought each other like savage jungle beasts, battling out the primitive matching war of the human animal.

Afterwards they fell exhausted onto the bed, and he felt the world fold in around him, dizzily, as if he were falling through an endless pit.

CHAPTER TWO

His words were still ringing in Ann's ears as she stepped into the living room of the apartment she shared with Mari Thornton.

"Is that you, Ann?" Mari's voice called out from the kitchen, followed by the clanking of pans.

"Yes," she answered falling down onto the yellow overstuffed chair that faced the large television screen opposite the front door.

"Had anything to eat?"

"Yes, Joe stopped off at a restaurant in San Bernardino." She felt a sense of tiredness and slight elation. The weekend had been marvelous.

Mari stepped out of the kitchen. She was dressed in blue stretch pants and an open topped blouse. Her figure looked quite fetching.

Ann fought down the images that pressed themselves on her mind at the sight of the other woman.

"Like Joe?" Mari asked.

"Had fun, if that's what you mean!"

"And?"

"He'll call, tomorrow!" Ann assured the other woman, smiling. "How'd your weekend turn out?"

"Nothing exciting. Old Lenville. Ralph, you've met him before...last week at Darvi's party."

"That tub?" Ann cried, amazed. "He has a stomach that would..." She laughed. "Crush you!"

"Isn't so funny!" Mari frowned, then smiled, adding: "He's important!"

"And...?"

"And...that's it!" Mari shrugged, and the action

15

moved her breasts under the white blouse. She stepped over to the chair and sat on the arm, her ankle touching Ann's leg.

"I missed you, Ann," Mari murmured, pouting her lips. "Ralph Lenville ain't the lovin' type!"

Mari's hand touched Ann's shoulder; it was a caressing touch.

"Don't!" Ann said, twisting away from the other's caress.

"What's wrong?"

"He worked me out pretty good..." She stood, moving away from Mari.

"You're a strange one, love." Mari's eyes were stripping her body naked, obviously picturing the upward curve of her breasts, the sweep of her rounded hips, the firm thighs, shapely legs. "I knew you like it with women...but can't understand you enjoying a man. With me...well, I do what I have to...and...well, sometimes it does work out. But a real soft woman—that's something!"

"Sex is sex, Mari. I turn on...when the lights are low, and the setting is sensual. I need sex! I have always needed sex!"

Ann picked up a pack of cigarettes from the coffee table in front of the low green sofa. "There's nothing strange about it!" she continued, after lighting a cigarette. Suddenly she felt like talking, about herself, about sex. Sometimes talking was almost as good as doing it. Some things were just as exciting when relived as with the doing. Ann knew her moods, knew that her body was too exhausted to go through the motions of love—but talking about it was something different.

"How about a drink, Mari?" Ann suggested, sitting down on the sofa, taking a deep drag of the cigarette. She watched the other woman move into the kitchen in a swivel-hipped fashion that lighted an instinctive fire within her. Mari's fanny was delightful to touch, fondle. That first night, when she had come to live with Mari, they had made love. They both knew about each other, through the girl who had recommended them to one another. The discovery of the intimate pleasures they could share had been a logical step, right from the beginning. They would be living with one an-

16

other for some time, and they had to know how they would stand, both emotionally and physically with one another.

Mari returned, sat down next to Ann, close enough so that their thighs touched.

That annoyed Ann.

"Drink up, love," Mari offered, handing over a stiff whiskey and soda.

Mari's hand lay down onto Ann's thigh.

"No...talking! Nothing else!"

They had played this game before, and in the short few days they had been living together, Mari had already learned about Ann's moods. The hand retreated. The woman shifted away, moodily, leaning her head against the back of the sofa.

The thrust of the woman's large breasts pushing hard against the cloth, attracted Ann's attention, then she drew her eyes away, looked at the blank television set on the other wall.

She sipped her drink, took a drag of her cigarette and waited. Mari would start her talking. In time.

The silence was long, then Mari finally sighed, said:

"Well, love, it's your party! You've made the ground rules!"

"I was thinking...about when I was loved up for the first time. A young boy, in high school, in the back seat of the car. Boy was he awkward! All he wanted to do was play breast games and then hop on. But...I guess it was good. Well, I didn't know any better!"

"It was a girl, first time with me," Mari put in. "She was older, and knew what she was doing. How wonderful she was. We did it a lot of times after the first one. I was...well, too young to know the full meaning...what was happening. It just felt good."

"I didn't know a woman until college. My roommate liked girls. I liked sex, came home one evening after a date which had fizzed out—the guy got too drunk to finish what he started and I was burned up in more than one way. I was wild, desperately needing it. This girl said she knew how to take care of the need—and boy! She really knew how!"

Ann sipped her drink, put out the cigarette and

17

lighted another, nervously. Suddenly she wasn't in the mood to talk anymore. Her thoughts were turning to Joe Dickenson. He had been good. A gentleman, and excellent lover. They had really swung through the weekend.

Ann felt Mari slipping closer and then the light touch of a hand on her thigh.

"No!" Ann snapped, angrily, standing, looking down at her roommate.

"I'm sorry, I can't help wanting you. You are just about the most lovely woman I have ever known, Ann." Mari's throat was husky, her eyes flaming with desire.

Ann felt anger whipping through her. "Cut it out! You know I don't want anything! Joe fagged me out!"

"Damned Joe!" Mari sneered, hatred tightening her face into a hard, cruel frown.

"He was good, Mari...very good. He knows how to treat a real woman!" Ann said, nastily, wondering at the emotional fury that suddenly burst through her.

Ann realized there was a mean streak in her, one that she had never really understood or been able to control. The sight of this other woman, so obviously desiring her flesh, created the urge to be cruel.

The expression on Mari's face was that of a woman who had been deeply hurt. She just sat there looking up at Ann, as if she'd been slapped.

But Mari said nothing.

For a long time they stood there, looking at one another. Then finally Ann sighed, said: "I'm sorry! I'm tired, like I said. Think I'll run off to bed. Tomorrow might be a busy day for me."

Downing the drink, putting the empty glass on the coffee table, Ann felt the deep guilt she always experienced after being unreasonably nasty.

She forced a smile on her face as she said goodnight to Mari, then turning started for her bedroom, closing the door behind herself.

* * * * * * *

Mari sat there, dazed, stunned.

18

Her body was aching to find the release of physical love with Ann Farrow. But already she had learned that the other woman was strange, demanding. Ann made love, wildly, completely; she lived life as fully. Just in the few days that was obvious.

She snapped up the still half-filled glass of straight whiskey she had poured herself, and took several strong swallows.

There was something about Ann Farrow that turned her on, fast. Ann had a body that might have been created by some artist with sex on his mind. Her face was clean, almost innocent looking. But there was a hardness, a selfishness in the woman that Mari couldn't understand.

She turned her thoughts away from Ann, and they reluctantly went inward.

Instinctively sparked by the obvious difference between herself and Ann, Mari wondered what had made herself more Lesbian than other women. She figured that it surely had something to do with the fact that her first sexual partner had been a very feminine Lesbian, a professional Lesbian, who knew how to seduce a girl and introduce her to the joys of female lovers.

There had been a lot of women in Mari's life—and a lot of men, since she had come to Hollywood. But the men were business. Women were pleasure.

As a young girl, Mari had touched onto the life of the prostitute for a few months, when down and out, after a three-month marriage that ended in divorce. Her husband had walked out and never returned, because she wasn't willing to bed down with him enough, and in his opinion, was a lousy sex partner. What Tom hadn't known was that he was a lousy lover, too.

With no money, working at a bar, Mari found herself in a position to be picked up, and when one of the other cocktail waitresses mentioned it was possible to get money from the pickups, Mari fell into the trap. That lasted a few months, until such time she had enough money to come to Hollywood and attempt her luck at being an actress. She studied hard, went around with the young actors and finally got connect with the "In" group, and saw the right people. It wasn't hard for a woman with her build to make friends. Most men liked big women, and she was damned big. Her breasts measured *45,* and men loved to prove they were all real, all her own. And she made the most of it with them.

It was nicer than being a whore, and paid off in a far better way.

Mari Thornton knew she wasn't a star, and knew there was little chance of becoming one, but she still liked her life. Plenty of party-time, more than enough lovers, both male and female. And some good parts from time to time to keep her active with the right people. Hollywood was made for a woman like her—both men and women made their plays and she enjoyed the benefits of these connections.

She made several movies a year, enough to keep her in food and room, and managed to room with women who liked a little Lesbian love on the side. That part was important to her.

The only thing that bugged her now, was the fact that Ann Farrow was something different, even special. For the first time in her life, Mari could think about something other than the kind of existence she had been living.

What that was, she didn't like to think about, and didn't even really understand. But there was something about Ann that caused her to feel more than mere casual interest.

She laughed, throatily.

Ann thought that Joe Dickenson would be really giving out with some important contacts.

Sure, Joe would play along with Ann, get what he wanted from her; and he even *might* give her a role or two—walk-ons, but nothing more.

Joe had troubles of his own.

What Ann didn't know was that she had introduced her to the man because Joe was a good friend, and because Joe would hardly be a threat to the nice little arrangement that the two women now shared together. Joe played the casting couch game to the hilt. No strings.

Mari felt guilty. She had led Ann on, told the woman that Joe would help her, really put her where her career would start out with a bang.

But Mari knew the real reason she was misleading

20

Ann. And she hated herself for it. Still, she had every right to do with her own life what she wanted to—and survive the best way possible.

Once, some months before, Ann had helped a roommate, really well and the arrangement had fallen through, with Mari sharing the apartment with nobody.

Mari stood, finished off her drink, looked at the closed door to Ann's bedroom.

"Well, I haven't been completely dishonest with you, Ann," she murmured aloud to herself. "Joe will help you along, but slowly, and you will work your way up, like I had to—and we will be together longer than you think."

She sighed, picked up Ann's empty glass and went into the kitchen. A few moments later she returned to the living room, moved to the closed door that held her away from Ann and stood there, tempted to go inside and seduce the other woman.

"No...I won't push things. There's plenty of time. It'll take a while before Ann really gets her big chance...and then—maybe it will be too late."

Startled by this spoken statement of her true thoughts, Mari realized fully what she was doing, what she had been planning on doing from the very beginning.

She really wanted Ann Farrow for herself.

"Why you little bitch!" Mari mused with a twisted smile. "Fooling even yourself."

With that, Mari turned, went into her own room, which was next to Ann's, closing the door behind herself.

CHAPTER THREE

Joe Dickenson stepped into the small office that had been given him at the *Bennick Studio* for casting, nodding to his secretary, June Swenson, a slender blonde with slightly buck teeth, but attractive features and eye-catching figure. He had made a polite pass at June once, but she had blocked it in no uncertain terms. Later he had heard rumors that June didn't like men—but nothing about her liking women, either. She was an excellent secretary and that's all that really counted.

"How are you, Joe?" she asked, smiling warmly.

"Anything interesting?" he asked, pausing beside her desk, before entering his own private little nook, which was partitioned off. "I mean, of course, outside of yourself!"

"Why Mr. Naughty Boy, shame on you!" she laughed. It was a ritual they both enjoyed.

"Anything wrong in flattering a man's secretary?"

"Just so its his, not some other guy's!" she laughed.

"Now, tell me whom ever would I possibly be interested in when I have you right here guarding the door to my private kingdom?"

"You mean casting couch, don't you?" she accused with a wink.

"Why, now, shame on you!"

"Not at all. You men are all alike."

"So are you women."

"That's not what you told me yesterday."

"Sometimes I lie."

"Well, to be truthful, you all look alike to us gals, too. Can't tell one from another, as the old saying goes!"

"Well, in the dark, anyway."

"You're really horrid!" she smirked in delight. "But fun to spar with—at arm's distance, of course."

"Sparring with you could be…interesting. Only, alas, you're taken."

"The hell I am!" she exploded more serious sounding than either of them might have expected. "Well, lets say, I'm not about to be tied down to anybody. I'm a free woman!"

"But a slave in the office."

"Yes, a slave to my master."

"And? To get back to the original question: Anything interesting happening, on my venue, in my immediate future? Or do I have to drink my coffee alone in my room, like a bad little boy?

"A call from your—ex-wife. She sounded…well, like it was important!"

"Okay, get her on the line." Joe went into his own little nook, closing the door behind him.

Beth Dickenson always had something of importance to talk to him about. He wanted to be finished with her. They had had a good life together, until she turned off sexually. Any time he had attempted to get close she had turned to ice. When he tried to talk about it, she refused, going into a tantrum. Or simply avoiding. Her sexual coldness had finished off their marriage, turning him toward other women. In his job there were plenty of willing ladies. The casting couch was a joke, but not a lie—it was there, like in any business. And in show biz it was a matter of showing what you had in order to get the business. And many men used their power to enjoy the free samples being offered all around. Until Beth turned off on him, he'd been Mr. Nice Guy. Since then, he'd managed to make use of his position to connect with women. Like this last weekend with Ann. She was something else!

As he sat behind the small desk, the phone rang. "Hello?" Joe said after picking up the receiver.

"Joe, I'm glad you called."

It was Beth, her voice high and nervous, anxious.

"What's the trouble this time?"

"You don't have to start being nasty!" she cried in a hurt voice.

"Beth…I'm a busy man and—"

24

"Don't tell me about that, Joe. I know about your *business!*"

"Let's not start *that* again!" he snapped.

"Okay."

There was a long silence, then finally Beth said:

"I have to see you."

"About your monthly robbery of my bank account?" he snapped, immediately sorry for his words.

"No...something else. It's important, Joe. Please. Dinner, tonight?"

He considered, remembering his plans to take Ann Farrow out on the town.

"Please, Joe. It's really important!" Beth begged in an anxious voice.

He thought about his ex-wife, and the good times they had had together, and how much he had loved her. The loss of their child at birth and the nervous breakdown, afterwards, had been the beginnings of their troubles. It was impossible to think about Beth without remembering how he had felt about her. They had had several good years together, no matter what had happened since. He still cared about her as a human being; even the bitterness of the last couple of years couldn't completely kill that.

"I can't," he finally said, fighting off the urge to say yes.

"I...*have* to see you!" There was just the tinge of desperation in her voice. That struck an emotional hammer in Joe. Beth knew him all too well.

"Can't we see each other at...lunch?" he offered.

There was a short silence, then she sighed: "I guess...if that's the *only* way!"

"It is!" he announced firmly. "The only way."

He'd given up a lot of time in the last period of their marriage, and he wasn't interested in losing any more—Ann was far too interesting and rewarding.

"Okay, here, at home."

Joe sighed as he replaced the receiver on the hook. He thought about Beth for a long time, annoyed that it was necessary to see her again. He wanted to forget everything they had shared together, but she kept coming into his life, reminding him of what they had lost. He needed time to forget the pain and the loss and the terrible emotional mess that had ruined their marriage.

Angrily he turned his thoughts to Ann Farrow. She was something completely opposite from Beth. Ann had been quite a delight and surprise. He had not expected it from the woman when first seeing her at the party Friday evening. She liked being close, intimate, was a wonderful sex partner. All movement, amazingly responsive—not like the cold, chilly Beth.

The phone rang.

When he picked up the receiver, a gruff voice shouted through it.

"Come up here, Dickenson!"

It was Walter Bennick, studio boss and owner, and from the sound of the man's voice, Joe knew that something was wrong, terribly wrong.

As he stepped past June's desk in the outer part of the office, he saw a trim little smile turn her lips upwards. She shrugged.

"Trouble?" she offered, knowingly.

"Damned if I know."

"I think its Carol Clements. They're having problems with her on the set. Hasn't shown up...from what I've heard...on time more than once. A real MM, if you know what I mean. And yours is the head that's going to fly!"

"Will you catch it if it comes your way?"

"What?"

"My head!"

She laughed. "Watch out for the hatchet man! He'll lop it off!"

"I know!" Joe sighed, stepping out into the hallway. Joe had been the one who recommended Carol Clements to the studio as a lead in the current Bennick film. The trouble with Carol Clements was that she didn't know a good thing when she saw it.

When Joe walked into Bennick's plush, huge office, he fought down the tight hardness that was grinding at the pit of his stomach.

"Close the door, smart-guy!" The huge man sitting

26

behind the large desk didn't stand. His face, fat with too much drink, glared at him.

Joe closed the door, stepped in front of the desk waiting to be told to sit. The order didn't come.

"Your idea, smart-guy. Get Carol Cements for *Roaring Guns!* Real good for the part. Sexy. Good actress. Just the part for her! She'll make the film, and we'll be making a star even brighter! That's what you told me. Now, see if you can get the film made!"

"What's the trouble?"

"You should know. I warned you, Dickenson. She has to stay in line. That's your duty. Carol has played the Big Star once too often. Either you get her on the set, and on time, or it will be your hide if this film isn't finished on schedule! We have a lot of money tied up in this project. Carol is playing her own game! I thought you talked to her Friday."

"I did. She promised to be a good girl!" Joe told his boss.

"She isn't! She won't answer the phone. You go out there and find out what's the trouble. And find out fast! I want her on the set, tomorrow morning, on time. We are shooting around her today!"

Walter Bennick stood, smashed a heavy fist against the desk. "Dickenson, you're a smart boy. Your idea about Carol was good...because she wants a come-back, still looks great and can act! We get her cheap because no other studio will touch her. Smart thinking, there. Now, you be a really smarter boy and see to it that she finishes this film—and on time! This is the last warning! I mean it. You want to be a producer; you want to run the whole show. I know—word gets around. Well, I've decided to give you a good chance to prove yourself. If we finish this film on time you can try producing the next one!"

Joe Dickenson stood there, dazed, hardly able to believe his ears.

"Don't think I'm giving you anything, Dickenson. I'm merely putting your job on the line, with a reward if you succeed in handling Miss Clements! Okay, boy?"

The man grinned, but it was a false, forced grin. It

was a dangerous expression, with narrowed, hard eyes.

Walter Bennick was not playing any games. He had a movie that needed finishing, and on schedule, because money was time and time was money and *Bennick Studios* couldn't waste any time or money. Plus the man was notorious for being Mr. Cheap. But it was a chance to jump forward in one leap; a chance Joe had never dreamed possible for some years in the future. Sure he had planned, hoped, thought a lot about it, and even talked to a few friends, like John Denton, screen writer.

Now that the chance was being offered he felt scared.

Either he got Carol Clements in line, or his job and future were finished. Everything would go! And his reputation would be shattered. Word would get around that Joe & CC had blown their chance.

His future was now tied into Carol Clements. And that would be like saying your life depended on the Titanic not sinking.

He sighed, tried to smile, said: "Thanks, I'll see things run smoothly from now on, sir."

"You better do just that! And I'm not kidding. Or you have no other job, as of now. Your full attention has to be with Carol and the finishing of this film, in twenty days!"

He wanted to gasp in surprise. Twenty days wasn't long.

"That means she'll have to be on time every day from here on in! Understand boy?"

"Understand!"

"And I don't care how you do it. If you have to stay with her night and day and have to leap into bed with…well, I know her rep. Everybody does. You screw her brains out, if you have to. I don't care what you do just so she gets here on time. Got me?"

"Got you."

"You're a lucky fella," the man chuckled. "How many men would give their left and right nuts to be in your position. Do you know how many men want to bed CC? Hell, she's a dream girl. She's the lady that men get all hot to fuck and that's what we're selling. She's selling. Well, on screen. In the flesh she tosses it around like cheap fish to be

28

given away before it rots. You're a lucky guy. Go play with those big titties of hers, if you have to. Bouncy, bouncy!"

The man roared with cold, nasty laughter. "

As he walked out of the office, he was already beginning to put some plans of action into order in his mind. With CC you had to play it smart and know exactly what you needed to do. She could be nice, warm and very difficult. She could turn her mood on and off like the flip of a coin.

Carol Clements was a lush, and a tramp, but most of all, she could be good box-office, and that was why he had suggested her in the first place.

Joe stopped by his office to tell June that he wouldn't be in for the rest of the morning.

The drive to Carol Cements' Brentwood home took over thirty minutes. It was ten thirty when he arrived, parking his car in the driveway.

Carol lived in a large two-story home on *Tigertail*, which was far too large for one woman, let alone for a star on the skids.

If Carol wasn't in, possibly her maid could give him information as to where he could find her. As he rang the doorbell, his stomach tightened nervously. Nobody could know what to expect from this dynamic woman.

He was running the ulcer road, and there was nothing else he could do. After almost ten years on the motion picture merry-go-round it was impossible to turn to another profession. It had cost him too much to get this far; he couldn't start over, even if he wanted to. The prospect of losing everything he had gained, just because of a broad who wouldn't cooperate, was not going to happen—not if he could help it.

The doorbell rang, and the dark haired maid stood there.

"Oh, it's you."

"Is Miss Clements in?" Joe inquired.

After a moment of hesitation the maid said: "I couldn't be sure. Earlier this morning she said she wasn't in for anybody, but...I know you got her a part in the film and...maybe you can be of some help. If I told you she might be in—but wouldn't let you see her—you might force your way into the house...out to the pool!" The girl smiled and

29

then slammed the door in his face.

Joe stepped off the front porch and then went around to the back of the house. There was a large wooden fence that surrounded the back yard. He reached over the gate and unlatched it, then went into the garden that covered part of the lot.

As he stepped around the corner of the large house, the bean-shaped swimming pool revealed itself.

A bouncy, fully-stacked woman was standing on the diving board, a flimsy bikini hardly covering the most interesting points of her body. A white swimming cap covered most of the jet-black hair.

A charge of electric excitement surged up through him. It was one thing to see Carol Clements on the screen or on the set—even in one of her semi-nude scenes, but quite another to see the woman in such a setting as this.

This was a dimension all of its own, a universe that was isolated. Total privacy.

As far as the world was concerned, they might be the only people existing. They were cut off from any view of the outside world, with only the maid in the house.

Carol leaped and then dove into the pool, slicing the water like a knife. But that one leap had bounced her breasts in a most inviting way.

Like Bennick had said: *Bouncy, bouncy!*

Carol claimed she'd never been enlarged, never gone under the blade like many starlets did. In face CC was quite proud of the fact that her body was real, all hers.

Stepping to the poolside, Joe waited until the woman surfaced.

"Hello, there!" he greeted.

Carol gasped, treading water, only her head and hands above the water line.

"Where the hell did you come from?" There was neither anger nor friendliness in her husky voice.

Those large, dark brown eyes peered up at him questioningly. Her pouty, firm lips were held half-open, water dripping from her rounded features.

"Your maid said you weren't in...so I took a chance!" Joe explained, grinning, trying to get a good look down the woman's bikini top, under the water.

"So—what do you want, Joe, Darling?" she grinned, her eyes brightening.

"You know there's a picture being made?" he inquired.

Carol didn't say anything, merely swam to the edge of the pool, slowly pulled herself out of the water and then stood in front of him, dripping wet, very close, so that her breasts almost touched him.

It was impossible not to remember the reputation that Carol Clements had.

According to Hollywood in-group reports, Carol liked her supply of men and had bedded down with almost every important movie-land figure.

The fact that she had never made a pass at him didn't effect his mental fancy.

She squinted up at him, because the glare of the sun was bathing down at her eyes. The squint wrinkled up her cute up-swept nose, pouted her lips, dimpling them at the corners. Several locks of black hair had worked their way from under the bathing cap, over her smooth, even forehead.

"So you're running to get me back on the set?" she observed.

"That's about it!"

"Wasted your time!" She stepped away, went down the poolside, picked up a towel, returned, handed the towel to him. "Dry me!"

It was a command, not a request.

His hands were shaking as he worked the towel over her wet body. He could feel the texture of her flesh, soft, supple, under the towel. When his hands came close to her breasts he backed off.

"You better do the rest, Miss Clements."

"What's wrong?" she teased, taking the towel, looking up at him knowingly. "They won't bite. I promise you! And they're all mine! Real woman! And you men…oh, you men love…well they're my treasures and my bank account, too boot!"

He merely shrugged and watched her press the towel over her breasts.

If it happened by accident or by design he was never quite sure, but when her towel moved away from her left breast, the bikini top had fallen below the nipple.

The sight of that pert, firm nipple, standing up hard against the oval throne of her firm, bouncy breast, was like a kick in his guts.

"Naughty nipple! Sorry about that. Don't want to tease and tempt you!" She giggled and pulled the bikini top up, covering the naked temptation.

"Why don't you go into the playroom, fix yourself a drink—me too, while I...as they say in B movies, get into something more comfortable!"

"You look pretty comfortable, now!" he managed to say lightly.

Her eyes questioned his, frowningly. "Wet suit!" was her only comment as she turned and walked toward the back patio that centered in the middle of the U shape of her home.

He stood there, watching her walk away from him in that famous swivel hipped fashion that had made her so famous in the motion pictures, each jerk of her fanny sending a needle of desire up through him.

For a long time he stood there, shaken, looking at the door through which she had disappeared.

Finally Joe took a crumpled pack of cigarettes from his suit pocket and lighted one with shaking hands.

Carol Clements was one sex-bomb who knew she was great and liked to spread her shock power over every man within sight. It was an ego trip and a game she played everywhere. But he'd never been alone with the woman like this. In CC's home. Anything could happen. That was obvious. She was in total control. And he'd been told to reel her in and land her at the studio the next morning at all costs.

He felt a sense of frustrated confusion.

To her, Joe Dickenson was a nothing; just one of the guys at the studio. She knew little of how he had worked to get the part for her; how he had fought with Bennick to convince the man that it was a smart move on their part to hire her.

Finally Joe moved toward the house, wondering how it would be possible to convince Carol Clements that it was very, very necessary that she be on the set each and every day on time.

He could hardly tell her the truth.

Threats would do nothing. Carol was a very stubborn woman who still believed in the fantasy that her name was magic and that every Hollywood producer was screaming to have her work on a picture. It was an illusion that she surely must have worked to keep alive; for any fool would have known the truth. The woman's reputation in the town was so bad that her career was entering the gutter scream of has-been. He almost felt sorry for her.

This was something he could not hit her across the face with. Her fury would be so terrible that it would take his career down the tubes, and chances are some other young upstart exec would be placed in charge of the woman. The studio certainly wouldn't just dump her now that she was under contract, as long as somebody could keep her line.

Sure, they might do that, but Joe wasn't about to dump his career if he could help it. All he had to do was satisfy the sexy woman—something which most men would find a delightful mission worth paying a lot for.

There were few men who would not jump to be in his shoes.

So he had to learn to play the game in a safe way, in a way which would involve being whatever Carol wanted him to be.

She was the Star and if she said jump, he'd have to ask how high.

PARLEY IN PASSION, BY CHARLES NUETZEL

CHAPTER FOUR

They had finished their second drink, sitting in the playroom, a large place created for boozing and playing any kind of games. There was a long sofa, which obviously opened out into a bed, on the wall opposite the large home bar. They were sitting in comfortable overstuffed chairs, across from each other.

Carol Clements had put on tight fitting slacks that looked several sizes too small around her rounded hips and thighs. The open necked white blouse, which gave a good view of the valley between her breasts, had taunted him for some twenty minutes, driving a natural, almost impossible reaction through him. She simply wasn't a woman a man could look at without feeling quick desire, raging passion, down right raw lust, even in a crowded room. In the intimacy of her home, sipping drinks, it was something overwhelming.

"You'll stay for lunch!" Carol announced suddenly.

"I can't—have an engagement!" he told her firmly.

"You'll break it, of course!" she snapped, the smile hardening on her face.

He considered, then sighed. "Okay."

There really wasn't anything else he could do about it.

"That's good. I like a man who can make a quick decision." She stood, left the room and a few minutes later returned. "Mable will fix up something good."

Joe stood, went to the bar. "Mind if I have another?"

"Help yourself, and fix me one more scotch—but straight, this time. I hate fooling around. And this isn't the time to fool around…well, not in that way… you know!"

She stepped up to the bar next to him, close enough

so that he got a good whiff of the perfume that she was wearing. It was sensual, like everything about Carol.

She handed him the glass and he filled it with Scotch.

"That should hold you some!" he smiled, half filling his own glass.

Carol tipped the glass over her lips and gulped, almost draining it.

"Think so?" she offered, gazing evenly into his eyes.

Shrugging, Joe started to turn from the bar but her hand reached out touching his shoulder.

"First time I really noticed you, Joe. You're not a bad looking guy!" Her fingers slid down over his arm, then squeezed hard into the muscle. "Nice, hard. Do you work out?"

"Well, just my natural self!" he offered, lying a little.

"I think I like you." Her fingers caressed and squeezed his arm again, lingeringly, sampling, considering. "Yes. Nice and hard…bet you're…well, never mind that."

She turned back to the overstuffed chair and settled down, stretching her legs outwards. The pose was sensual, arching her back, straining the blue cloth over her hips.

She teased him with a wink. "Like what you see?"

He shrugged as if indifferent. But the way her eyes literally stripped his frame, pausing meaningfully at his groin for a moment sent a hot fire down his spine.

"I think you like what you see," she observed, then smiled knowingly at him.

After a moment of lingering silence she asked in a strangely serious voice.

"Want to talk about it?"

He gaped at her, not quite certain what the question meant. Connected to what she'd just said it was full of erotic implications. But her tone of voice indicated something totally different.

A stunning shift, change of topic.

For a moment the question floated in his mind, without any meaning. Some how it guessed that the woman was playing a special, nasty game with him, allowing her words to flash a double meaning. The pleased expression in her eyes as they continued to brazenly consider him was amused.

36

She knew he was turned on fully by her sensuality. But, then, most men were, unless they were gay, he concluded. So CC shouldn't be too surprised by that. Nor overly pleased. He was, in reality, just falling right into her lap. Like every other man she tempted, teased and in many cases used to satisfy her own personal needs.

"The picture," she offered, apparently aware of his confusion And she made no effort to hide the fact from the expression sparkling in her dark brown eyes, that she knew exactly how confusing her mixed message had been and how turned on he was. The woman knew exactly what he was thinking. This was a scene she'd played out too many times with too many men to expect differently. It was all automatic with CC. She ran her little game-script and watched the sucker bite into the obvious bait.

"You have to understand the studio's point-of-view," he told her carefully. "They have a lot of money invested in the film and...they depend on you to be there for a day's shooting. We can't afford to run over schedule on this picture."

"So...?" she sighed, sounding bored.

"I'm serious, Miss Clements."

"But bored." She sighed. "Please call me Carol," she added, almost as an after thought.

"Okay, Carol...a lot depends on you cooperating on the film."

There was an edge of desperation in his voice and she didn't miss it.

Her eyes flicked to his, seriously.

"Where do you fit in?" she demanded bluntly.

There was a long silence, then Carol suddenly burst out laughing. Her breasts bounced, shaking.

"What's so funny!" he said tightly.'

"*You!*" Carol finally burst out, controlling herself. "I bet you are being made into the fall guy! I bet Bennick put your job on the line. And I think that's funny!"

She laughed again.

"It isn't funny!" he announced, controlling the fury that threatened to explode.

After a moment Carol sobered, took her drink,

downed the rest, stood, went to the bar, refilled the glass.

"Well, what should I do?" she inquired, leaning back against the bar. Her breasts pushed out against the blouse; her hips were thrust forward.

Everything Carol Clements did seemed to be a sexy pose, designed to invite a man's passions to rage out of control.

"Report to the studio every morning at six, until the film is finished."

"Why?" she demanded. "Why should I put myself out for you?"

That question choked at his throat. The anger flared up, trembled up past his lips.

"Who the damned hell do you think you are?" he yelled, suddenly standing in front of her, so close that if he leaned forward her breasts and hips would be touching him.

He didn't know how he had gotten so close, but the sudden nearness was almost too much to stand.

She sobered quickly. For a long time there was no expression on her features. For a moment he held his breath, expecting to be ordered out of the house.

Then she said, seriously: "It's that important to you?"

He nodded.

"And as for who I am, I'm a star. And don't you forget it. Maybe there have been some difficult times in the past, and some pushy crumbs have given me a lot of trouble. But I'm a human being, no matter what people might think. I'm a woman, and I'm lonely, and in a lonely profession. I can't find a man who will make me happy for life. I'll probably never get married again, because it is hopeless to try. I'll fail in that. The only thing I have is my career. I work hard. I must live up to the Star image. And nobody, but nobody tells Carol Clements what to do. If the studio has to pay a little more for my services—that's just part of the game I don't care. I'm the star, and they can cater to me. I had to cater long enough to a lot of slobs with fat hands that couldn't keep off my breasts and fanny, who wanted to know if my body was for real!"

The outburst came so fast, that when it ended they both were stunned.

38

Finally Carol sighed, turned away from him, helped herself to another drink, downed it and refilled the glass.

"I'm sorry. But it's been coming for a long time. I know what I am—but Hollywood made me that way." She faced him, smiled. "So, lets not talk about serious things. I want to get to know you better before we get back to business."

Carol ran a fingernail along his cheek. The touch was like electricity. She smiled, her lips parted, moist, moved close to his. Then she twisted away, as if having changed her mind about something.

The maid came in some time later and announced that lunch was ready.

It was that which startled Joe into remembering his luncheon date with his ex-wife, Beth.

"Can I use the phone?" he inquired.

"Sure, behind the bar."

Joe moved around the bar, picked up the receiver, dialed, waited

Finally Beth's voice said: "Hello?"

"I can't make it this afternoon," he said, without even announcing who he was.

"What?" Beth's voice shouted through the receiver.

"I'm sorry...something came up and it was impossible to—"

"One of your women, no doubt!" she snapped.

"Oh, come on, Beth, this is business hours."

"That never bothered you when we were married!"

"Anyway, even if there was a woman involved, it has nothing to do with you any more! I'm sorry. This is business and—"

"Business before pleasure!" she snapped.

There was a long silence and he could hear her heavy breathing through the receiver.

"When, then?"

Joe said, without thinking, "Tonight?"

Silence, then: "Okay."

The line went suddenly dead on him.

Carol Clements smiled as he turned and faced her.

"A luncheon date with another woman?" she inquired.

"Ex-wife."

"Then I don't have to be jealous, do I?" she said throatily, stepping up to him, taking his arm and leading the way to the dining room. That first contact sent an electric surge through him. She might have felt it, too, but showed no reaction. She was being casually intimate, as if they were simply old friends.

It was a simple lunch, according to Carol. But to Joe it seemed more like an, elaborate dinner.

Salad, wine, Shrimp Cocktail, thick, juicy steaks, boiled potatoes covered with butter and onions, with wine to go with it. After the main course there was Brandy, generously offered in large brandy snifters.

During the lunch, Carol questioned him about his wife, his past, his childhood, his career.

He told her about growing up in Hollywood, going to college, majoring in Theater Arts, his stint in the army, in Germany, his return to Hollywood and long struggle to get into the motion picture business.

"And your wife?"

"Beth came in just after the Army," Joe said, sipping the after-lunch brandy.

"And what went wrong?" she dug.

He shrugged. "What usually goes wrong?"

"Sex or love stopped. I think it might have been sex!"

"What makes you think that?"

"A man in your position gets a lot of offers. I made enough in my time to men like you. They took me up on it, too." She shrugged, swallowed hard on the brandy and then took a cigarette from the little box on the table. She waited while he lighted the cigarette for her, then said: "You're good looking enough. A woman would be a fool to jump out of a marriage—without some good reason."

The liquor and meal, the atmosphere worked on him and he said: "Beth lost her...baby and...well, after that...I guess she was afraid of getting pregnant."

"That's a bitch. All of it. And, also, that last, that's bullshit. *That* can certainly be taken care of—unless it was against your faith."

40

"Nothing like that...but I have a theory about it!"

"Don't *all* men?" she mocked. Then shrugging said, "And what are your future plans?"

"Production, I guess." He let it lay there.

They were silent for a long time and then suddenly Carol stood, started from the room.

"Come on, Darling." Her voice commanded. He followed like a faithful dog, hypnotized by her swaying fanny. And wondering exactly what she was leading him to. Nothing was obvious about CC. Other than what she attempted to show off in an obvious way. But there was no second-guessing this woman.

She continued on through the living room and then into the playroom, closing the door behind them.

"Well, we are alone." She stepped close to him, slipped her arms around his neck and pressed tightly against his body. Her lips hesitated only long enough to position themselves under his.

The kiss was sharp, biting, her lips soft, open, her tongue demanding its way deep into his mouth.

Then she pulled back, stared at him, and moved to the large sofa.

"And you want me to return to work every morning at six. And for that...you get—what?"

She sat there staring across the room at him, all business.

"That's my problem."

"I'm making it mine!" she announced firmly.

When only silence met her statement, Carol said:

"Come on, if you want my help, you better level with me, Joe—and fast!"

"Bennick said he'd move me up to production if I could—get you in line."

She frowned, then sighed, a deep sigh that lifted and dropped her breasts.

"What do I get out of it?" she inquired.

"A good mark."

"I don't need it...I'm a Star! They have a contract, and they can't break it!" She studied him. "Maybe I should be a good little girl. But I don't want to be—not yet!" She patted the sofa, said: "Why don't you think of some way to convince me there's some reason to help you?"

The implication, at least the way he was reading it, seemed to be an open, raw invitation.

"Come on, don't be afraid of me, Joe. I might be a star, but I'm a woman, too. A woman who has, natural hungers and desires, a woman who dreams and is usually lonely, because everybody has their own ideas, about me! You'd be surprised how men can be. They think of me as...well, something to use and throw, aside. I'm more than that. Surely you realize this!" Her voice was deep, husky with passion. Eager lights fired her dark eyes, like burning fires in black, watery pools. Stars in the night, silently pleading with him.

"You want a favor, Joe. I want something, too. I have hungers. I have needs. And you might not believe it, but...well, to be blunt and frank: I am lonely, right now."

He could hardly believe that a woman like Carol would be lonely.

Possibly the expression on his face revealed his doubt.

"It doesn't matter," she told him, "why I'm lonely. But I want companionship—the most basic companionship. Sit down beside me, Joe, and let me find out what kind of companionship you can offer. If it's good enough...I'll be more than willing to make it worth your while. After all, I'm a beautiful woman. I know that. And men desire me. I know you, now. I know what makes you tick. I know the kind of man you are. I like that. I like the kind of man you are, Joe."

He stepped over to the sofa and she reached up for him. Her hands circled his forearms, the fingers squeezing, feeling the firmness of his muscles.

"Come on down, Joe, and show me what kind of companion you can be to a real woman. When you've shown me, I'll give you my answer."

There was hot promise in her eyes as he settled down next to her.

Carol's fingers slipped to his hands and pulled them to her breasts.

"I'm kinda hot for you, Joe. Can you believe that? You should. Well. Right now I'm hungry...and real hot. I

42

hope you know how to handle a fiery woman. I certainly hope you know how!" Her lips were close to his, her hands pressing his fingers against her breasts. The perfume attacked his nostrils like sensual magic.

But he didn't need any magic to desire Carol Clements. Her body was all the magic any man might desire. It wasn't love, only raw, needy passion without strings, without demands other than the feeding of itself.

CHAPTER FIVE

Carol's hot breath breathed against his throat as he worked the blouse off her shoulders. She sighed, bit his earlobe when his fingers found the clasp of her bra and freed her breasts for his searching hands Her nipple hardened tight under his palm and she pulled his other hand down to the zipper of her stretch pants.

"Hurry, take them off," she breathed, tonguing his ear, lifting her hips to urge him to faster speed.

He caressed the slacks off, caressing her firm thighs, teasing her to franticness as they slipped over her knees and finally over her ankles.

She had been wearing nothing on under the pants and now he felt the sure fire of passion drive him wild at the nakedness of the woman.

Carol drew him tightly against her, covering his face with kisses, squirming, locking her legs with his.

Her own hands were already beginning to help him remove his clothing a moment later when they broke from the hot embrace. In a short time they held each other tightly together, stretching out onto the sofa, full length so that their whole bodies were put into play.

She sobbed, gasping as her hands drew his head down to the lush heat of her large breasts.

It was like attempting to hold down a tigress gone wild. She moved on the sofa as if an earthquake were shaking her. The sounds, animal, savage, brutal, kept coming from her throat as he made love to her body.

He had known a lot of women, and he hardly felt anything other than a heated, drunken passion for Carol, but even in the greatest depths of the union of their bodies, Joe knew a desperation he had never experienced before.

Carol was a tramp, a cheap, whoring woman, willing to give her body to all men; but more than that, she was a woman, and for the first time, he realized, a very desperate, anguished woman.

As her nails dug deep into his back in that last moment of ecstasy he tensed against the combination of pain and pleasure.

They fell away from each other, exhausted.

After some moments, Carol lifted from the sofa and left the room.

He lay there, thinking, wondering about the woman who had just ordered him to make love to her.

It was that, and he knew it.

Strangely enough his thoughts turned almost immediately toward Ann Farrow.

Ann was younger, sure—possibly ten years younger. And her body was certainly no more beautiful from normal standards. Though with Ann it had been something different than with Carol.

He lay there for some time trying to think out the difference. He hadn't resolved it in his mind by the time Carol returned.

She slipped down beside him, leaned close, touched his lips with her own.

"You were good, Joe," Carol announced, lying down on her back, looking at him.

Her breasts were still high, peaked, even though she was lying on her back. She winked, teasingly.

"I think you'll do fine."

After a moment of silence, Joe asked: "For what?"

"My lover! That's what."

That startled him. He hardly thought of her as a lover.

He immediately compared her to Ann Farrow. Both were a new experience, within the same time frame. Both, at this point, casual connections, without emotional ties. Yet both amazingly desirable woman. Both apparently enjoyed being with a man and enjoyed sex with a lustful passion.

Then he thought about his wife, Beth, whom he had loved, lived with for years, and divorced. That woman was cold ice compared to either Carol or Ann.

The last couple of years had been hectic ones. After the divorce there had been several serious affairs. But not until Ann Farrow had he considered any woman more seriously than for a one night stand or bed games for an extended period. Nothing serious—period!

He suddenly realized that he had planned on really helping Ann in her career, in a serious way. Open doors for her. Strange that he could feel so totally captivated.

Carol grinned. "You'll be my lover—and I'll be on time at the studio."

His head spinning, Joe stood, dazed.

There wasn't anything so terrible about her offer, just one hell of a lot stunning about her casual statement, as if this were a business deal concluded.

"You don't like the offer?"

He shrugged. "It's your party, Carol. Simple as that."

"The ground rules are you come to me when I call. Okay?" she demanded, face bright.

Suddenly Joe Dickenson felt the ground pulled out from under him. Carol Clements had managed that.

She was in total command and knew it and literally rubbing it in—making it as obvious as possible. Cut. Dry. Calculated. A business deal.

Any man would jump at the chance to have an affair with such a woman, just for ego sake. But to be commanded—that was something else.

Joe turned and looked at the woman, puzzled. She had said she wanted love, romance. Oh, not in so many words, but that was just about how it was spelled out.

This wasn't romance. This was prostitution—male prostitution.

Carol was grinning, and the expression in her eyes was all-knowing.

She was fully aware of what her command meant, and the meaning it had over him.

There wasn't any way out.

"Oh, come on, Darling, it can't be that bad, can it?" Carol cooed, letting her eyes run the full length of his body. "I'm the dream fuck of every man alive. And you're getting me on demand! My demand. But what man wouldn't just beg for such a chance? Be a sport and enjoy. I sure plan on doing just that!"

He forced a grin.

"See, you do like me...just a little. So enjoy. Will that be very difficult for you to do? After all, I'm the dream-girl you're selling to the world. And I'm all yours, at my beck and call. That can't be too ... well, demanding on you. Now can it?"

"Hardly," he managed to say.

"Come over here again, I think I'm just about in the mood for another sampling of your companionship. You're such a hard man, all over. I liked that. Liked it a lot. Give me another sampling of your...hard love. Love."

* * * * * * *

Ann Furrow came home from work at the restaurant, edgy, annoyed.

"Any phone call for me?" she asked Mari who was putting the finishing touches on dinner.

"None."

Ann sighed. "Joe was supposed to call me."

Mari's voice was shadowed, as if she were holding back emotion. "You can't be depending on any man in this business."

Ann went into the kitchen. "You can stop being so smug!"

Ann stopped short.

Mari was dressed in panties, the rest of her body naked. The woman turned, her breasts large and inviting. "I wasn't being smug, love."

Ann recovered. A feeling of amusement settled over her. Mari was clever; she had to give the girl that much.

"Aren't you cold?" Ann suggested, leaning against the kitchen table.

"Why?"

"Well..." Ann nodded to her naked condition.

"Oh, it was hot!"

Ann smiled. "How about Joe's phone number."

"I gave you that," Mari announced, taking a plate and starting to put food on it. Her back was turned, but not quite enough to hide the upturned point of a breast.

"I mean his home phone number."

"Oh, love, that'll do you no good. You can't chase a man like Joe. He has a lot of women."

"None like me!" Ann announced, harshly.

Mari turned, glared at her for a moment, then smiled. "Maybe you're right."

She brought the food over to the table, and they sat down to eat in silence.

Ann found it difficult to keep her eyes off the other woman's breasts. They were lovely. She couldn't deny the woman was very sensual. Men must find her lush breasts quite inviting. Hell, even she felt a tease rush down her spine—too sensual.

"How'd things go with you, Mari?" Ann inquired.

"Danny hasn't come up with anything. But thinks he might have a reading next week."

"What'd you do today?"

"Hung around the apartment. A little boring. I just kept thinking about you, Ann." Mari put her fork down, looked at Ann so meaningfully that a chill rushed down her spine.

A sinking feeling attacked Ann as she remembered the sensations of this woman's body, those soft silk of supple breasts cushioning themselves against her own, the silken flesh...

The image was erotic and the feeling far more exciting than she liked to admit.

Of all the years she had experienced sexual relations with other people, the Lesbian exercises were still somewhat new, and uncertain. She liked pleasuring men, liked sex on many levels, even with women it could be enjoyable, but she favored men. Oh, she was adult enough to understand what such actions really meant. Having Lesbian lovers didn't make you a Lesbian. Any more than having Negro lovers made you a Negro, a Japanese lover made you Japanese. A caress was a caress, a thrill, a thrill. It was all just a matter of difference—once you had learned to accept it that way. Plus the norm might be more a liberal sprinkling of bisexuality with a heterosexual preference for most people. Cultural breeding and conditioning dictated a black and white, yes-no, attitude about such things. But the world was becoming more sophisticated and at the same time actively anti-everything different and new.

At this point in her life, she was experimenting between lovers; not involved with any man on a serious level and trying hard to get a focus on a career. This was what had brought her to Hollywood in the first place.

They finished dinner in silence, but the looks that Mari was giving her all through the meal meant only one thing.

Without a word, Mari pulled down a bottle of vodka, made two strong screwdrivers, and handed one to Ann as they went into the living room.

Ann knew exactly what was going to follow. It was logical. They were at home, alone, with nothing planned for the evening. And, as with a man and woman, the situation had become sensual in nature, and as with a man and woman, it would develop to its logical conclusion.

But she sat down on the over-stuffed chair, in order to hold off their "logical conclusion" a little while longer.

She thought about Joe Dickenson, and realized she knew very little about the man. He was her mark. That party had proven that. She knew exactly what she was doing—but still felt a deep frustration that the effect of their weekend outing hadn't been as strong as she had expected. She would have to find a weak spot in the man, and play on that. All men had a weak spot. She would play him.

Mari broke into her thoughts with: "What're you thinking?"

"Oh, about Joe, and what to expect from him."

"Oh, he's like all of them. Stupid. All they want to do is dick a girl."

"Maybe. I'm not stupid," Ann stated, annoyed.

"I noticed. You're smart enough to know exactly how to drive a man right between your ... lovely legs!" The woman laughed at her crude joke.

"That's nasty!"

50

"Of course it is. And right on the spot!" Mari laughed, crassly. "I'm not a fool, either. I know what makes the world go around. And I know what turns me on."

Ann looked away, nervously.

"You turn me on, you know that," Mari's voice murmured very softly.

Ann ignored that. There was a long silence.

Her thoughts drifted away from Mari and the implied intimacy the woman would demand soon enough.

Ann admitted to herself that she wasn't afraid to do anything to get what she wanted. She wanted a start in movies and had been told that the best way was to sleep with the right people. Not all the people, but the right ones.

The trouble with most of the girls who came to Hollywood was that they thought all you had to do was throw yourself at all the possible male helpers along the way, and certainly there would come a few who would help make you a star.

Most of them ended in the gutter, or lost, or prostitution.

There were too many women willing to climb in bed with VIPs. Men used such women—and didn't give them much in return—if anything.

She sat there, looked at Mari, thought: *Now take you, Mari, you put out to a lot of men, and where are you?*

And, interestingly enough the woman really didn't like men that much.

The perfect example of a woman who didn't really know how to use men; but certainly knew how to be *used* by the men.

"Tell me about Joe," Ann asked. "You know him better than I do."

"I told you all there is to tell. He plays around. Likes a woman who shows him a lot of loving. If you're lucky he'll give you a start—open the first door," Mari said, annoyance in her voice.

"That's not what I meant. I mean about his personal life."

"Oh, come on, love, I don't know his personal life! I'm not a father confessor! He was married. Divorced. His

51

wife was a cold fish. They loved each other, I guess. That's all I know."

"What about him? What is he after in life?"

Mari laughed. "Getting women to spread all their goodies out for him to taste! Like any male prig!"

The woman gulped her drink, patted the sofa next to her. "Why don't you stop the chit-chat and...try being more friendly."

Ann sighed, sipped her drink, then angrily gulped. The Vodka was strong and burned her throat. Finally she stood, slinked over to the sofa, settled down next to Mari.

The other woman, more basic, already driven to a point of strong need, placed a hand on Ann's leg, then boldly lowered her fingers until she had reached the bottom of the skirt. A moment later the hand caressed upwards, under the cloth.

CHAPTER SIX

Joe looked at the woman he had been married to for several happy years.

They were sitting in the dining room, of the house that he had bought, and was still paying for; eating ground round patties, mashed potatoes and string beans. Beth Dickenson, a slight girl with a sensitive face, full mouth and large blue eyes, stared across at him, smiled slightly, then looked down at the plate of food in front of her.

She was dressed in a low cut blouse and full skirt. Her small, jutting breasts pushed against the tightly fitted blouse, accenting their firm but small shapes.

They had talked about little of importance since he had arrived, merely covering the normal social conversation which two people will go through when they are playing out an awkward scene.

Joe had been at the house only a few times before, since the divorce, and only once for dinner like this.

He wondered what she was planning to ask him for. Usually it worked out this way.

The frantic call, the invitation for dinner, then the request. Last time it had been for more money. Debts were piling up and she had needed a thousand dollars to pull herself out of a financial bind.

Later, after he had given her the money, Joe learned the debts had occurred because she had used a lot of money in Las Vegas. It was a habit acquired in the last few years, after their marriage broke up.

It was hard to look at Beth without feeling the emotions that had prompted him to marry her in the first place. She was such a wisp of a girl, so helpless seeming, but so able to fight her way through the world's jungle.

"How did the 'business' appointment come out?" Beth inquired, after finishing off her meal.

"Fine," he answered too sharply.

His nerves and body were sexually exhausted by Carol Clements' physical demands. Twice hadn't been enough and he had come to the conclusion that it would never be enough for Carol. She had a body that just craved men and sex more than any one man could respond. In the end she had finally ended up drunk, half-conscious, and a little angry because he couldn't respond to her needs.

"The office said you were at Miss Clements' home," Beth announced almost angrily.

"What?" he cried, startled.

"Oh, I'll admit...I was angry and..." Beth shrugged.

Joe almost said something biting and nasty, then remembered it wouldn't do any good. An argument would only make things more difficult.

"Would you like a drink?" Beth inquired, standing.

"No—I'm a little bushed, and...I don't want to eat and run, but...it was a hard day."

She smiled icily. "I bet it was!"

They went into the living room in silence. It was a cozy place, and Beth was a good housekeeper.

When he settled in the sofa, Beth moved down next to him, much too close for comfort.

He looked at her and saw that the second top button of her blouse was unlatched.

An accident, he thought, tiredly.

"Joe...I'm..." She sat there, her hands, small and child-like folded in her lap. Her voice was thin, almost frightened. "Joe...I've been thinking about...*us*."

A long silence followed.

Then she stood suddenly. "Are you sure you won't have a drink?"

"Sure."

She rushed out of the living room and it was some time before she returned. There was a large glass in her hand that contained what looked like straight whiskey of some kind.

That surprised Joe, because Beth had never been much of a drinker. There was a glazed expression in her eyes, as if a strong jolt of alcohol had already slapped her nerves.

She sat down next to him again, her thigh touching his.

"Joe...couldn't we start over?" she blurted out suddenly.

It was like being hit in the face. He sat there dazed, unable to believe what he was hearing. It wasn't like Beth. He could hardly believe she was serious.

For a long time he couldn't think of anything to say. Nor did he know exactly what he wanted to say.

"I'm...I mean it, Joe. I've thought a lot about...well, these last...two years have been long...they've been long ones for me, Joe. I've learned a lot about life—I've changed a lot, Joe. I'm not the little girl you married—and I...I've come to terms with myself—as a woman...if you know what I mean." She gulped the drink, turned, stared into his eyes. There was a desperate, frightened look on her face.

"I know it's sudden—but we did have a good thing...until—well, it was my fault that you...saw other women! If I'd understood how important sex could be to a marriage, I would have...no! No! I wouldn't—then! I have changed, though, Joe. Believe me. I just can't continue this way!"

Tears were suddenly streaming down her cheeks; her face was flushed, her lips trembling.

She sat there, staring at him, not saying anything for a long time, as if waiting for him to do something or say something.

He didn't move.

It was like watching a movie, but one that had full shock value in a very, very personal way.

He couldn't move. Couldn't even think logically.

Everything was happening too fast, too illogically to absorb it all.

He was thinking about his own personal life, his immediate problems, the life he and Beth had shared, and trying to tie them all together into one unit. But nothing fit.

Nothing went into an organized pattern. It was all like a jig-saw puzzle with half the pieces missing.

Two years ago it would have meant something. But things had changed so drastically for him since then.

Beth was not a part of his future plans.

But that didn't mean she couldn't be.

And that idea startled Joe, too. Because he had constantly fought to keep her out of his plans, out of his future. The long struggle had been hard, but in the end it had worked out well for him.

He lived a bachelor's existence; and he planned a future producing movies, romancing women, and making life the best possible one he could.

Marriage had failed one time; and in the failure, his ability to really love a woman had been damaged.

Maybe, he thought, because it was impossible not to still love Beth. He had loved her the first day they had met, and even when seeking out other women to sooth the physical desire, when they were still married, he had loved Beth.

"Joe, I still love you...I need you desperately." Beth sobbed, still not moving.

"Beth...oh, Beth...what can I say?" he stammered.

"Tell me you love me...please Joe...love me. Let me prove I'm a woman. Let me show you how good it can be in my arms."

She suddenly moved, throwing herself at him, covering his lips with kisses.

Stunned, Joe sat there frozen, unable to move. Then finally when her arms slipped around his neck, he did the wrong thing. It was partly motivated by emotional shock, but also by exhaustion.

Gently, but firmly, Joe pushed Beth away from him. She didn't struggle. For a long time she sat there, gazing down at her hands, which had fallen to her lap.

"Beth..." he finally managed to say, struggling for the words. "I don't know...what brought this on...but...I just don't know what to say." He was standing now, looking at her.

His head was swimming. He felt as if the world were spinning around him. The drinks of the afternoon were already beginning to wear off in a dully-painful way around his skull.

He didn't know what he felt for Beth. It just wasn't possible to absorb what she was saying and what it could mean to his life. He could only think that this was all impossibly insane.

"I'd better go," he finally said shortly, turning and starting for the front door.

"To your other women?" Beth blurted out.

"No," he said gently.

"Please, Joe...please give me a chance!" She stood, ran toward him.

"Beth, this isn't the right time!" he argued desperately when she threw her arms around his neck.

"I love you, Joe. I have to have you. I can't live without you!" she sobbed, shaking against him.

It seemed like a scene from a B-movie. It was all too unreal for him. The emotion raced upwards and the bitterness burst out.

"Damn it all, Beth. Stop this. It's just too damned late for this kind of thing!" he yelled, cruelly pushing her away. "Too much has happened!"

She stood there, staring at him, her face white, eyes wide, lips compressed

As he reached for the front door, she said: "A lot has happened...too much that you...don't understand!" But her voice was dead of emotion. Joe opened the door, left the house like a man chased by a ghost. A panic, an unreasonable terror had taken control. All he could think of was getting away from the house, away from the temptations which it offered.

* * * * * * *

Under Mari's caresses, Ann was forgetting about her anger and concern over Joe Dickerson's broken promise to get together with her that evening.

Mari had skillfully worked the skirt upwards and finally even pulled it off completely after caressing madness in Ann for the physical union of passionate bodies making love.

Mari was a good lover, one of the best Lesbian lovers that Ann had known. She seduced her with skill and tenderness, knowing exactly how to excite the fires of passion.

It wasn't long before the two of them were completely naked, stretched out on the sofa, locked in a hungry embrace.

The pressure of Mari's breasts against her own was exciting and pleasant. Then suddenly the woman was caressing, kissing Ann. The kisses ran the extent of her throat, down over her shoulder, to the mound of her breast.

It was like floating on a sea of pleasure, feeling the kisses, the caresses, so skillful, so knowing.

There was a difference between a man's and woman's love-making. Where a man was forceful, demanding, driving, and able to give a real woman the final satisfaction of deep voluptuous ecstasy, a woman was genteel, instinctively finding *all* the areas of excitement, and playing out the foreplay to the fullest. All that was missing was the final act. But the buildup was as good, if not better, than most men could give a woman. And it was so different.

She waited and the caresses became too voluptuous to endure. Then her body went through the anguish and searing pleasure of ecstasy.

It was only Mari's words that ruined the full effect of the love making.

"I'm crazy about you, Ann. I love you. I know that. I want you forever." They were statements expressed in the heat of desire and the heat of emotional fire.

Ann felt as if she had been slapped in the face, hard. Her body went cold and rigid.

Those were words, which no woman should say to another. At least not to her.

Sex was sex. But...love? Never from a woman. That was something else.

The coldness chilled through Ann and she felt the desperate need to run and never stop running from Mari .

There had been a frantic conviction to those words of love.

Anybody could tell when truth had been expressed in a moment of passion. And those words were sobbed from the

58

very soul of Mari.

Ann sat up finally, lighted a cigarette, moved from the sofa, walked to the large bay window and looked out over Hollywood.

Mari was silent, as if guessing what had been said was too much—a very bad mistake.

There was no use for the woman to deny that she meant what she'd said. They both knew it. Ann turned finally and stared at Mari's naked body, a feeling of contempt and disgust sickening her stomach.

"I couldn't help it," Mari cried in desperation. "You are so lovely, so wonderful. I love you and I'm not ashamed of it!"

Ann started to say something, but then discovered a hard lump in her throat.

"Please understand, Ann. I won't demand anything! I just want to love you!" Mari was pleading, begging, face contorted in fear. "Please, just love me…that's all I need. Please, Ann…please…" The chanting voice seemed to be moaning like a horrid mantra. "Please, don't…"

"Oh, shut up! Enough!" Ann snapped. "I don't want Lesbian love."

"You liked it. Be honest! I'm good. Better than any man could possibly be with you. And you should have heard your moans and groans. Don't tell me I didn't really give you the best time you ever hand. You were gasping and pleading for more and more, you couldn't get enough of it. You're just like me. But you won't admit it!"

"Oh, shut up!"

Mari stepped closer, now within reach. "Don't be stupid, Anne. I know you liked me. I know you want me. I'm better than any man!"

The woman leaped at her, arms flying around her neck. For a moment the two of them clutched together, unmoving, frozen in time. Then suddenly Anne screamed, and pushed the other way.

"Come on," Mari challenged. "I'll give you—a real thrill!" Then the woman reached out, almost furiously pressing the palm of her hand up between Ann's legs. "I'll make that so hot you'll scream in joy."

"Oh, Christ. You slut!" Ann pushed and slapped at the same time, her hand raced across the other woman's face. It wasn't a hard blow, almost missing, but made the point. "What's with you? It's just been for kicks."

"Kicks?" Mari sounded shocked, hurt, puzzled.

"Yes. I'm sorry, but..."

"Sorry?" The word was spat out in hard fury.

"I...it's been a mistake. I didn't mean..."

"Take that and shove it deep!" the other woman fairly screamed in fury.

"I'm not one of your kind! I'm a *normal* woman, who likes a lot of sex—but...this is a lark—just something to do when there's not a man around!"

"You cheap slut. Calling me a slut. You're a cruel, nasty woman! I hate you."

"Oh, go to hell!"

With that Ann went into her bedroom, slamming the door behind her.

Suddenly she felt cheap and dirty for the first time in her life. Real cheap and real dirty. She had been cruel to Mari, but the woman had been demanding and pushing her just too far. It had been a mistake, right from the start.

"Oh, God, how do I get myself into these kinds of things?" she moaned, hands covering her face.

* * * * * * *

Mari sat there on the sofa, sick inside. The damage was done and there wasn't anything to do but face it.

Somehow she had to make things good. She did love Ann. That much she knew for sure now. From the first time they had made love to each other. But it had been too fast then, too much happening.

Now for the first time in her life, Mari was in love— and she had obviously picked the wrong woman.

Then a strange feeling settled over Mari. Maybe, if given enough time, Ann would change. Ann liked sex with her. The woman's body really responded to the caresses. And Mari didn't fool herself about her ability to make love, to man or woman. But with men it was like prostitution—

with a woman it was love, and beautiful and exciting.

She stood, went and fixed herself a stiff drink.

Somehow she would have to think of something. And she would, if given enough time.

PARLEY IN PASSION, BY CHARLES NUETZEL

CHAPTER SEVEN

The tears had washed away for Beth Dickenson and drinking had replaced them.

She lay on the sofa, the hi-fi playing *Wagner* at full power, the room darkened. How long Joe had been gone, Beth didn't really know. She didn't even know how long she had stood there in the middle of the room crying or how long she had been drinking. Time had a way of telescoping and drawing out in irregular patterns when she was drunk.

Beth rolled over on her back, reached awkwardly toward the coffee table for the drink that was standing there, but instead knocked it over.

The contents of the glass fell to the rug, spilling out. For a moment she felt regret because of the mess the spilt drink would make, then her voice cursed out:

"To hell with it all—damned it all, all the whole world!"

The voice was thick and slurring even to her own ears.

You're drinking too much, Beth! She thought, tormented.

But then she had been drinking too much for some time.

Funny how people changed. Take herself. Before she had been married, she had believed that sex was for marriage and for only one man that the vows of love were forever. She had never had a man before and didn't know anything about sex because her family just didn't talk about that subject.

Oh, she knew where babies came from and how they were made. She knew what a man was supposed to do to a woman to get her "that way". But it was merely a scientific knowledge.

Joe had taught her everything she had known. He had shown her what it felt like to feel a man becoming a part of her. She had thrilled to his love-making, believing that no man could do anything like that to her. It was love—wonderful and beautiful.

Then the loss of the child, and the fear that she would never be able to have another child ruined everything. The confusion that had caused her to fear sex made things impossible. But she hadn't known the truth about men.

Joe loved her. He wouldn't want to touch another woman. After all, sex was merely the outgrowth of love. It was that way with her. Surely it was the same with him.

There had been the arguments, sure. And he had subtly warned her about the facts of life and men.

"I love you, Beth—you know that. I desire you. I want to hold you in my arms, and make love to you. A man needs a woman that way!"

But love was more than just sex. You love me. I love you—that doesn't mean we have to have sex-parties all the time!

Not now, Joe. Not tonight, she had said once too many times.

Then one evening the telephone rang and he said he wouldn't be home until late. Business. Monkey business.

That continued until one evening he called, and a woman's voice had sounded over the receiver saying:

"Hurry big boy—baby wants some more of what you got to give her!"

That had been the finish.

Sure, he shouldn't have slept out on her. But on the other hand, she should have understood how desperately a man could need a woman. She hadn't lived up to the bargain. Marriage was a two-way street and she had put him in a position where the sexual side died or he found it elsewhere. In his line of work there were just about unlimited women willing to climb into bed with a man who might help them in their career.

The ruin of the marriage had been shattering to Beth. After several months living alone, she went to Las Vegas with a girl friend of hers, and learned from that bachelor woman what a real female did for kicks in a wide-open town.

They had drunk themselves silly, but never completely smashed, that first afternoon. Done a lot of careful gambling, won some and had dinner at one of the shows.

At the show they were sitting next to several men, alone. Conversation ended up with two of the men offering to pay their bills and suggesting they come to their hotel rooms for a few more drinks. Ruthie, Beth's friend, led a lot of the conversation. Ruth was a good one for getting men to pick her up. She knew all the tricks, how to flirt in a continually open manner that invited joking and then serious steps to seduction.

Beth had seldom drunk in her life, and boldness had come over her at the drift of the conversation, boldness of being in another town, where nobody really knew her, mixed with the consumption of so much liquor.

The idea was exciting.

The two men were sharing a suite, which had two bedrooms, ideal for men on the make for willing women.

First the drinks, then when one of the men turned on the radio, Ruth started doing a wild dance to the throbbing music playing. One thing led to another, after enough drinks had made them pretty friendly, when Ruth started undressing. It was a sexual tour-de-force, and it even excited Beth in an abstract way. She wished it was herself doing the strip dance, and that she was doing all those things to the tall, blonde haired man who had paired off with her.

And suddenly Beth let all hell break loose and started dancing with Ruth. It became a wild, erotic battle, each trying to be sexier than the other.

No doubt it was quite a show for the two guys, who ate it up, laughing, encouraging them on to greater fits of sexuality.

Then Ruth, who had been at it a little longer, stopped, sweat glistening over her now naked body. After a moment she went to her man and fell in his lap.

Beth followed the example, even though she had her panties still on.

Somewhere along the way they started making love,

all in the same room.

It was a dirty, filthy party; a wildly exciting evening and Beth felt cheap about it for a long, long time.

After they had come back to Los Angeles, Beth had never seen Ruth again, but had, many, many times, gone to Las Vegas, ending in some hotel room with a pick-up.

Until now. And what had happened to her.

It was to be expected. And in a way, Beth had felt almost good about her condition; gaining a strange voluptuous thrill at being so punished.

And she had turned to the only person in the world she knew that could possibly help her.

"Oh, God," Beth shouted, *"What am I going to do?"*

She couldn't have the child without a husband. That she could never face. Even if it would be possible to claim it was Joe, that he had made love to her and gotten her pregnant. She would know, and so would Joe. Unless she could seduce him.

That had been her so desperate plan. At least seduce him. But somewhere it had all gone bad and instead, she had pleaded with him to remarry her.

How foolish can you be! She wondered, furious with self-hate.

In the drunken state of her mind, Beth resolved to try again, to do everything within her power to get Joe to reconsider marrying her; then, if that didn't work, at least get him to make love to her. That might turn the trick.

Because, she realized, *there could be no life for her, otherwise.*

To have the child without a father she could at least respectably name, or to have an abortion, would be too great a sin to face.

Death seemed the only other answer. And that was a sin against God!

But she would try, once more. One last time.

One final, desperate last try to save face, save her life, save the life on the child in her, to save respect and...

Her mind faded then, dipping down into welcomed unconsciousness.

CHAPTER EIGHT

Two days had passed since Joe had seen or heard from his ex-wife. Most of his time off had been spent with Carol Clements, playing to the tune of her demanding passions.

There were less pleasant ways to pass the time, but Joe still felt a deep sense of uneasiness about his role in that arrangement. It all mixed with his confusion and concern over Beth's offer, it blended against a background of guilt and concern had made everything seem distant and dream-like.

Why had Beth suddenly become so sensual? Did she really want them to start over?

At one time that would have been all that he would have wanted, a chance to make it work with them. Now it all led to confusion. Ding-donging his mind. Maybe he owed her a chance—maybe he should try to fix things between them.

But could Beth ever be the woman he needed? Could she really ever turn her frigid sexual needs into a fire that would make her a real lover to a man? To her, sex wasn't all that important, never had been—certainly she hadn't changed over-night.

Yet a part of him wished it was possible.

The morning of Thursday, when he came into the small office, June Swenson looked up, smiled, said:

"There was a call from a young woman, said you had met last week-end, left her phone-number." There was a twinkle in June's eyes that teased knowingly at him. "You being a naughty man?"

"I'm nothing but pure and innocent. Have I made you

pregnant, yet?"

"Oh. Is that what you wanted to do? I had no idea!" She winked and then shivered slightly. "Oh, what a delightful idea. And I thought you believed in protecting a little lady like myself."

"You're more than a little lady."

"Well, maybe I'm a man in sheep's clothing."

"There's nothing sheepish about you."

"Ah, but I don't sheep around."

"That's sleep!"

"Oh. No wonder I never find the right man. I always get that all confused." She laughed then shrugged. "Guess I'll just have to take out my dick...oh, oops, meant dictionary."

They laughed hard at that and he said: "Guess you win today's battle of words!"

"I always win, just sometimes I let you think you've won. That's what a smart lady and smart secretary does, you know. Play up to a man's ego."

"Okay, now, back to the phone message. Who was it, what was it and—?"

"The lovely lady...yes, she was lovely, at least sounded very lovely. She said that maybe you had misplaced her phone number. Said you had told her something about getting together Monday night...something like that." The amused smile on June's face caused a moment of embarrassment to shoot through Joe.

"Oh, yeah," he mumbled, shrugging. Then he went into the inner office, settled down on his desk, and stared at a script that had been placed there the night before.

There was a note attached to it, from Walter Bennick.

"Joe, see if there's a part for a cute little blonde, big proportions, snappy personality in this one. Have a girl in mind for a part. Call Johnston and see if he could adapt one of the roles for the girl."

It was signed simply with a huge "W.B."

Joe opened the script. Then closed it, lighted a cigarette, sat there, thinking, gazing at the door across the desk.

He mentally pictured Carol Clements' nude body, as it had been the night before in the pool.

They had swum for some time before Carol came close to him, at the deep end and flung her arms around his neck. Their slippery bodies had ducked under the water, and as he was beginning to gasp for breath, Carol's mouth covered his.

The kiss was deep, passionate. Her whole body arched against his, her legs tensely embraced in a viselike hold.

As they broke the surface again, she gasped, laughing and teased him with her body.

What else could a man wish for?

He could wish for love, romance, a future with a woman who was worth loving.

If only Beth had been like this.

Carol Clements was not that kind of a woman.

Annoyed, Joe opened the script and began reading.

It was some time before the image of another woman flashed before his mind.

Ann Farrow. Blonde. High breasted, green eyed, voluptuous and sensual. A woman who was good in bed. A woman who had been a ball for two wildly exciting days.

Lighting another cigarette, he wondered why she should come to mind. He remembered the conversation with his secretary. But that wasn't good enough.

There was that curious peaking of interest, the fiery spark that lighted every time he remembered Ann. They had clicked. And he had looked forward to seeing her the very next day, but things got in the way. And business always comes before pleasure. Especially when the business involved pleasure. There was no doubt that the magical power of CC in the erotica department.

Finally he forced his mind back to the script. After a few moments the mental image of Ann Farrow returned to his mind.

Suddenly he realized why.

The lead girl in the script had taken on the face and figure of Ann Farrow.

Automatically, Joe reached for the phone on his desk. He buzzed June, said: "Get Ann Farrow on the phone."

It was a long time before June was able to connect

him. "Had to get her at work," she explained through the intercom.

"Hello, Miss Farrow—Ann," he said into the receiver.

"Yes who is this?" The voice was impersonal and distant, tired.

"Joe—Joe Dickenson."

"Oh, I was wondering when you would call. I called your secretary this morning, thinking you had forgotten...well, to be honest, I'd given up, and thought maybe it was all right for a girl to chase a man and—"

"That's all right." He was silent for a moment, suddenly wondering why he had phoned Ann. Then automatically he asked, not knowing anything else to say:

"Are you doing anything this evening?"

There wasn't any hesitation in her voice when she said: "No."

"I'll pick you up at—when are you free?"

"Any time after six—well, make that seven, time for a girl to change and get looking her best."

He chuckled, said: "Okay, seven. For dinner. See you then."

Without waiting for her to say good-bye, Joe hung up the phone, stared off into space, wondering why he had put through the call. What was his mind thinking of?

What if Carol Clements called—wanted his stud services for the evening?

Christ, studding for the Star.

He felt a mixture of anger and frustration. And automatic erotic pleasure. There was no doubt that out: CC was great in bed. And great in the ego department. How many men wanted to do just what he was being commanded to do?

And how many had already played that role at her demand?

To hell with Carol!

His eyes looked down to the script in his hands. For a long time they weren't focusing on the writing, but still mentally picturing Ann Farrow.

Ann was a most attractive woman.

A needling of excitement teased him at the thought of

70

making love to Ann. And you couldn't take such a woman to bed without calling it making love. She was beautiful and such a wonderful sexual partner. It was a making of love. A worshipping of the female body. And more than that. As little as he knew her at this point, he wanted to know her better. Instinctively he knew she was very special.

That, he planned on doing. It was going to be a nice change from Carol. A very nice change, if things were like they had been over the weekend.

For a long time he sat there trying to figure out what the difference could possibly be between Ann Farrow and Carol Clements. They were bodies; female sex-pots. Each equated a sex-party. Nothing more. Yet he would far more rather be with Ann than with Carol.

Maybe it was a matter of power? That simple.

Carol enslaved him.

Ann was enslaving herself to his will. No, that wasn't true. But it was a mutual partnership between them.

Carol was mistress of the deal and a very demanding, selfish one at that.

Maybe that was the difference between the women.

Carol was demanding his services.

Ann was giving her services.

Possibly that made the difference. And possibly it had to do with something more basic than that. Maybe two people met, and something clicked. Maybe it had to do with something sub-conscious in nature, that the outward mind couldn't logically understand. The old "soul mate" thing. He had never put much credence in that concept. Yet it sure as hell would explain his fascination with Ann.

It was some time before he was able to turn his attentions to the script. A little before lunch the phone rang.

Picking it up, Joe said: "Yes?"

Carol Clements' voice spoke through the receiver, saying: "Darling, how are you, today?"

"Fine," he answered briefly, mentally cursing himself for not having instructed June that he wasn't in for Carol this day.

There was that tremor in the woman's voice, indicated far more powerful than words, why she was calling him.

"I was wondering about tonight, Joe. Maybe we could have a Bar-B-Q outside in the patio. I *did* love last night's little pleasures, didn't you?"

"Sure, it was wonderful," he assured her in a tone that he hoped would sound convincing. "But about to-night...I'm afraid its out!"

"What?" It was a shout that blasted in his ear.

"Believe me, Carol...I'd give anything to say yes. But something of a personal nature has come up and—well, I just can't break it," he said firmly.

There was a long silence that screamed in his ears and then suddenly the receiver was buzzing dead.

Slamming the receiver down on the hook, Joe stood, went into the outer office, said: "No more calls from Carol, today. I'm out!"

June looked up worriedly.

"I know—but there's a limit to a man's pride!" With that Joe left the office, heading out of the building for his car. He needed a stiff drink, and time to think.

A deep depression was settling over him as he got behind the wheel of the car.

Everything should be perfect. What else could a man wish for? A lovely woman that all movie-fandom was desiring, throwing herself at him, demanding him as a lover; the career as a producer right in his grasp; even the past life he had lost with Beth being offered back to him on a silver platter.

Why couldn't the world be simple? Why couldn't a man's emotions work logically?

But there was something terribly wrong about his present situation, and try as he could, it was impossible to really put his finger on it. Maybe life had just worked up into one twisted, complex ball.

He tried to remember what he had wanted in the beginning, when he was just struggling to find his way in life.

A home, kids, a wife, family! Then things had gotten all twisted up, complicated. Divorce, the future turned upside down and now his life as a struggling bachelor, casting director with a promotion in sight, a future assured of success.

72

As the car pulled up in front of *Nelson's Steak House*, Joe relaxed mentally by thinking about Ann Farrow. She was outside his span of personal problems, and because of that—if nothing more—he was very much looking forward to seeing her.

The woman was already becoming an island away from the horrors of his real life.

* * * * * * *

The evening, so far, had been delightful. No passes. Mildly social conversation. A nice dinner, cocktails, and now dancing at the Hilton. And the pressure of the man's body against her own felt so good that Ann wanted to cry.

The last couple of nights had been trying ones for Ann, on several counts. For once in her life she was looking back at the past that had brought her to this place and time, thinking about the full future, not the immediate one.

She wanted to be a Star, to have her name in lights, but there was a lot more to life than that, and in these days she had been forced to face this truth. At least part of it.

The announcement, which Mari Thornton had made that Monday night, was still ringing in her ears like a voice of doom. For though she had played at Lesbian love herself, Ann had never been one. It had all seemed more like a little game, a lark. When there wasn't a man around there could be fun and games with a woman. Nothing more complicated than that. The words of endearment from Mari had shattered that fantasy.

It had been difficult to keep from going out to a bar and picking up a man Tuesday night. And Wednesday, Ann had actually gone to a bar, drunk herself to a raging hangover and almost picked up a man. The need to prove to herself what love was really like with a male partner was strong and powerful; too strong to easily control. Her hangover, the need for a man, and the professional need to build her contact with Joe Dickenson, had caused her to make the phone call to the studio.

Now she was feeling the man's body pressed against her own as a reward for that bold, forward movement.

Joe was so tall, so strong, and she could feel the strength of his desire for her as their bodies moved against one another on the dance floor. The music was slow and lilting, and her mood had suddenly seemed to shift slightly. She felt him pull her closer, the soft brush of his manly lips against the lobe of her ear.

"You are beautiful, Ann," he murmured, giving her body a little squeeze. "I can't keep my eyes off you."

"I should hope not." Ann said lightly.

As the music came to an end, Joe led her back to the small round table where their drinks were still sitting half finished.

After settling down, opposite each other, but only two feet away, Joe stared into her eyes.

"This has been a wonderful evening," he announced in a husky voice.

"And I hope it has only started," her lips said invitingly.

There was a long moment of silence. Then he pulled out a pack of cigarettes, offering her one. As they sat there quietly smoking, Ann was thinking about what would be happening that evening, wondering why the idea of being touched and loved by Joe Dickenson should suddenly have taken on so much meaning, so much importance.

Oh, she reasoned, *it might be because of her need for a man, and the desire to burn out for ever the taste of Mari's words of love.*

Ann knew that in a very short time she would be moving out of Mari's apartment, that they couldn't continue living together. It didn't matter that Mari had not made any passes at her since Monday night, or that anything unpleasant had gone on between them. In fact, Mari had been lovely and very much fun. But the relationship was finished. And most of all, Ann was sorry that it had ever started. It had to end.

But she had to wait. Make the right move.

"How about a ride down to the beach." Joe offered, suddenly breaking the silence.

"Sounds nice. I've always liked the beach."

They finished the cigarettes, then downed their

74

drinks. Ten minutes later they were driving along Sunset Boulevard, through Beverly Hills. The road was dark, almost empty of other cars. Most people were already in bed, or at least getting ready for bed. Thursday wasn't the kind of night for late staying up. Too many people had to go to work.

Ann thought about the job at the restaurant, and the early hour she would have to report to work. She considered it and then rejected the thought. That job was of no real significance. Right now the only thing that was of any importance at all was what would happen tonight, and the result of that event. These hours could be the door to her future.

She wasn't fooling herself that Joe would be hopping with excitement to do her favors, just because they were having an affair of sorts. The affair had started out from the first moment they had looked at each other. It wasn't a love affair. It was raw passion. And how many women tossed their bodies on his bed? She was certainly just one of so many that none really mattered at all to him. Just another body to screw around with.

But then, she realized there wasn't any reason it might not turn into an affair.

Instinctively she felt there was something more than just casual sex—momentary passion. Why? She simply could guess.

People were known to meet, go to bed the same night, fall in love, and even get married. Many successful marriages had started out that way.

That thought startled Ann. Surely she wasn't planning on trying to trap him into a marriage? That was down right childish and silly.

She turned, looked at Joe, and considered the idea of marriage. It wasn't an idea that came very naturally to her. A career just didn't mix with marriage! At least, not at her stage of the game. Here she was, in Hollywood for only a little over a month. Hardly anywhere. No agent. Just Mari, who had been willing to help her out because they both had a mutual friend.

She had no business even thinking about marriage. There was so, so much to do in the next few years. She was one of the lucky ones to be able to attack the inner circle of

Hollywood so fast. How many young girls had come into town and never even given *one* chance. Too many. And some of them ended up selling out a promising career for the married life. That was, of course, better than the gutter or street prostitution so many fell into. Or a job as a waitress or secretary.

Marriage was what parents did. It was for building families.

Such thoughts flashed through her mind and faded away. She fought them down and tried to center all her awareness on the moment. Nothing else, really, existed.

Now, as one spiritual teacher had told her, was all any of them had.

It seemed only a short time before they were driving along the beach road. Up the coast, the ocean breeze created an atmosphere of relaxation and peace.

"I've always liked coming here," Joe said dreamily, "Especially when...well, things were unsettled in my personal life."

Ann looked at him, saw a tense, nervous set to his features.

Restlessly, he continued talking. "I shouldn't be talking to you this way, but somehow I feel like talking...to someone. Why you, I don't know..."

His words, strangely enough, made her feel tenderly warm inside. He was offering her trust—a valued gift people only share with friends.

Or...

"Maybe because we're basically strangers?" she implied, lighting a cigarette, taking a deep drag. She hoped it wasn't that shallow.

"Maybe. But...things have been unsettled in the last few days." He shrugged. "No—no use ruining a nice evening. This is too beautiful to ruin."

He turned the car off the road and parked it so they were overlooking the ocean.

They sat there for some time, watching the ocean, dark and foreboding, softly splashing its way up the shore, onto the sands and then sucking back into blackness of the night sky.

Joe turned, stared at Ann, said: "You *do* have an effect over me. I wondered why I called you—I guess I know now. It was fun over the weekend—in fact, more than just fun." He was now very close to her, his arm slipped around her shoulder.

"Ann," he continued, "You're like an island on a stormy ocean!"

Maybe under different circumstances she would have laughed at what he had just said. But there was something about the expression on his face, the tone in his voice that made it a very beautiful statement; an important statement.

Then suddenly his lips were on hers, open, demanding, his arms straining to hold her closer.

She felt the cupping pressure of his hand on her breasts and a wave of excitement overcame her.

His tongue probed deep, hungrily into her mouth.

When the embrace broke, Joe looked suddenly confused. Without a word he started the car, turned it around and began heading back the way they had come.

"What's wrong?"

"Nothing," he said half to himself.

A long silence, then Ann asked: "You aren't taking me home, are you?" There was just the smallest edge of desperation in her voice. The last thing she wanted to do was go home.

He turned, looked at her for moment, and then nodded.

They drove until he stopped at a cocktail lounge. After parking the car, Joe said: "I'll be right back."

Some minutes later he returned with a bottle of whiskey in his hands.

They were both silent until he had driven about a mile and pulled up to a motel that was on beach front property.

"I hope this was what you had in mind," he announced in such a strangely harsh voice that Ann felt sure something was terribly wrong.

It was too late to turn back now, though. She patted his cheek. "Joe, I'm not a tramp, but...after the other day...honestly, I've been looking forward to this...being in

77

your arms."

Joe laughed lightly. The tension broke away. "I guess it is the same with me."

She was tempted to ask what had happened, but stopped herself.

They got out of the car, went into the motel. It took only a few minutes to get a room.

When the door had been closed behind them, Joe turned on the light.

"Well, it isn't home, but it will do," he laughed.

The motel room was small, with a big king size bed taking up most of the space. But there was a feeling about the place, which she couldn't quite understand, that made it seem the most wonderful room in the world.

She moved close to the man, looked up into his eyes and felt emotion sweep through her.

What was happening? She wondered, as his arms folded around her body, drawing her close. *This wasn't the way it was supposed to be!*

A sex party was nothing more than two human animals taking each other. Hammering away at one another like savage beasts out to satisfy a raw, bestial need. And she didn't really feel that way at all about him.

She didn't feel like taking, she wanted to give. That was something new for Ann—something strange and disturbing.

He held he for a very long time, just breathing against her. The two of them were clinging more than merely embracing. It was a lingering moment in time when souls met in some special shared space, merging together in a very quiet way, breathing against one another, uniting their very life rhythms, as if literally becoming one in some magically unreal way.

She felt his heart against her own and found the beat matching hers. They were like two parts of a machine being plugged into one another. A sexual union would not be as intimate nor as total. This was something other than mere physical connection; it was more like uniting into a far more powerful unity. They were surging into and throughout their mutual space, joining. And discovering the rest of what they

78

were all about. Together, rather than merely part of a whole.

It was a strange, new experience. It left her drunk in a totally new sense of awareness, as if some mysterious door had opened up to envelop the two of them, then closed in around the feast that was now being totally devoured in some wonderful Cosmos that had never, previously, existed for either of them.

They merely stood there, locked tightly together, clutching ever closer. Her mind opened up to embrace all of him.

Then his lips were on hers and her tongue reached deep into his mouth, tasting the wine there, thrilling, hungry to be as near as possible to this man. Searching for the very soul of his being, wanting it to become part of her, to *be* a part of her, to *be* her! She wanted to enclose all of his being into her soul. And it had nothing at all to do with sex. And everything to do with it. And had everything to do with nothing else but that delicious sensation of two bodies merging into one continuous unity of creation.

A tremble ran through her as he pulled away, went into the bathroom to get glasses.

She stood there dazed, stunned, breathing in the air of the room, but feeling as if she were breathing in the soul of the man who had just held her so completely.

Yes, she thought, *it was good that they would take their time. It was good that the drinks would come first. And maybe words of affection—and love.*

But were words even necessary? Could they ever express what she had just experienced?

And was that love? Or something even more deeply vital?

She shuddered at the thought, because suddenly that was what she wanted from this man. Words of love. Pale though they might be—they were the cement that could lock the two of them into some kind of mutual confession of the binding nature of their very beings.

How foolish! She told herself. *You're being romantic, silly, a child, dumb. Not mature. Not smart. Not sane.*

And I'm crazy mad about this man!

Then he was sitting down next to her on the bed and

they were holding glasses filled with whiskey and water.

"Ann, I don't know what's happening, but something is truly happening," Joe told her in a thick voice. His hand was on her thigh, just resting there. "I feel so different about you. Different than I have about any other woman for a long time."

Stupidly she said: "Oh, I bet you tell all the women that lovely line."

"No. Never."

"You sound...almost convincing," she managed to say with a tender smile. "Very nice, really."

"It's not a line."

When she didn't respond, because she didn't know what to say, frightened to reveal her own confusion and feelings too soon, he added: "I don't know if I like it—but..."

"Now you're...frightening me!" she managed to laugh.

"Never that...Oh, Ann..."

Then he wasn't talking any more because his lips were covering hers, his hand caressing the back of her neck.

Yes, Ann thought, thrilling to the tender wildness of the embrace, *something really was happening. And at the very time it should never, never happen.*

And she wanted it to happen more than anything else in the world. All else fell away as meaningless. Being with him, becoming a part of him, letting him enter her whole being, not only physically, sexually, but spiritually, in total, was all that counted.

She wasn't really aware of much more than sensation, floating. At some point she felt a bed against her naked flesh. But awareness of such details were blurred in a distant reality that had little to do with what she was actually feeling, experiencing.

Now was all they had. And in this moment they were all that either of them could ever be, together. For nothing else existed outside of their embrace. It blended them into a furious surge of mad passion, fusing all that was and ever could be into one fiery furnace of mere energy that totally consumed them.

* * * * * * *

Mari threw the glass against the wall in a fit of frustration and looked at the empty room, feeling a terrible sense of loneliness and anguish.

"Damned, damned it all!" she screamed, staring at where the glass of whiskey had smashed into the wall, where the liquor had dripped against the furniture.

She would have to clean it up.

Without much thought as to what she was doing Mari, automatically began to clean the mess, but her mind was centered on the image of Ann Farrow.

The last days had been hell for Mari, wanting Ann, and not wanting her at the same time. There had been women in her life before, many, but none had effected her in this way.

Ann Farrow, in some way was different from the other women and Mari was reacting far too strongly.

She was falling in love, something that had seemed an alien emotion to her. It was foolish, and silly and desperately needy.

After all, you loved your father and your mother—and if you had children you were supposed to love them. And a husband—or wife...but another woman, when you were a woman?

She knew there was nothing wrong with that, not in her world.

Yet there was a part of her that was standardized US-of-A morality, small town narrow-minded. That was her roots.

But was this kind of love she felt for Ann the kind she wanted to feel? It wasn't what so-called normal society classified as proper, correct and acceptable.

Oh, Mari knew the answer to that. She had always known the answer. There had been women who had claimed to love her—really love her as a man might love a woman—but it had all seemed a little silly. You made love to a woman, but you weren't supposed to be *that* way about it. Jealous and demanding. Possessive.

She tried to remind herself that one never owned another person. It was impossible to own something that wasn't freely given. At least in the emotional levels. Life was so damned complex.

If she could simply have been like her parents had believed in normal things. If she had only been like them. If she could have only fallen in love with a man, become a mother, wife. If only...

But that wasn't normal for her. Never had been.

Mari finished cleaning up the mess the broken glass and whiskey had made, then went into the kitchen. A few minutes later she returned with a bottle and new glass in her hands.

Sitting on the sofa, after having turned on the radio, she gulped several swallows of whiskey, wanting to burn her thoughts away from the desire that Ann Farrow created so deep inside her.

Where had she gone wrong? Really? There was no reason she should have turned out so...sick!

Yes, Mari thought, *she was sick of life and of the kind of life she led.*

She hated being different. Hated the woman she was. Hated not being able to share the dreams of other women for husband, children, and marriage.

That wasn't her. She was different from many so-called normal people. She lived in a shadowed world which society considered, at best, freakish. A world with little easy love, little ability for self-love, a world which preached narrow-minded hatred for something different from the average, the acceptable, the so-called heterosexual world.

She had this life, enveloped in confusion and supposedly shame. And she hated that. She wanted self-love and love like anybody else. She had needs that went beyond stuffing her mouth with food or gulping down booze until her mind blurred out. She had sexual needs that drove her towards women. Men were pigs, but a necessary business to deal with if one wanted a career.

So she lived in this shadow land that was so full of pain and anguish that colored all the other terrible agonies which everybody knew—the struggle for mere existence in a cruel world.

And she tried to make the most of it.

But what else was there to do? What else could a person do but live to the best of their ability? She had managed to survive. She had prostituted herself in too many ways, yet had managed to have some kind of success.

Hell, she was better off than most young girls were.

Mari emptied her glass, refilled it and gulped. Then her right hand unbuttoned the white blouse. She slipped her fingers under her bra, and burned for Ann.

She had to have it out with the woman. Things were getting impossible. Ann wouldn't give her body to Mari. That just wasn't right!

Yes, Mari told herself firmly, *When Ann got back, they would have it out and settle things...for good. It was just too much. Too damned much being so near, and yet too far to love and caress and...And she needed Ann more than any other person in the world.*

And she would have her...or else!

Mari stood, slipped out of her blouse, skirt, then pulled off her bra, stepped out of her panties, then started for her bedroom, staggering slightly from the effects of the drinks.

Once in her room, Mari stood before the full-length mirror on the back of the door, staring at her naked body.

"You have a good shape. Men love your body... women want you, too. So what is Ann's complaint?" Mari asked herself, thrusting her breasts out, admiring their hugeness, the taut nipples that were hurting with the want of a caress.

She knew, but didn't want to know.

Her hands cupped her breasts and it felt good, but at the same time hurt all the more.

Cursing, Mari went into the living room again, turned the music on higher, turned off the lights and felt her way to the bottle of whiskey that was on the coffee table in front of the sofa. She tipped the bottle over her lips and gulped.

It would be good to get real drunk. So drunk that she couldn't feel any physical sensations. Only that floating down the river of liquor, like a boat with no direction, in the darkness which would fold around her total conscious awareness.

A throaty laugh choked the room and Mari promised herself once again that when Ann Farrow came home there was going to be some real loving, no matter what it cost. Not even if she had to rape the woman! With that thought, Mari sat on the sofa, and took another swallow of whiskey, as the world of reality began to slip away into a blur of sensual feelings. Her hands caressed over her naked flesh, touching, sensing, caressing, imagining it was Ann loving her, wanting her, bringing her to gasping orgasm. Only in the final moments was Mari able to enjoy the exhaustive black nothingness.

CHAPTER NINE

To Joe it seemed so different being with Ann Farrow that he found himself confused and just a little frightened.

Her body was like ivory, silken, and beautifully molded. The shape of her rounded, high breasts were so full and firm, their rosy peaks so eagerly erect that it was more like making love to a Goddess, instead of a woman.

The contrast between Ann and Carol Clements was overwhelming.

When they had kissed in the car, a feeling of doubt had jarred his mind and emotions, and in an instant he had wanted to run away. It was a panic button without logic. But emotion had touched him; the kind that he didn't want to experience.

She lay on the bed, now naked, as himself, ready for his caresses that would bring her down the road to full and complete ecstasy. The look in her green eyes was haunted, mirroring his own inner puzzlement and need. This was different from what he had expected to feel this evening. Sexual desire, but not emotional need.

His hand reached out, cupped a molded ivory mountain, and caressed its rigid peak.

She squirmed slightly.

Strangely, after that sudden embrace, and the undressing, a passionate study of caresses, it didn't seem the right moment for wild erotic passion.

A wave of tenderness engulfed Joe, and he slipped down closer, embraced Ann, pulling her close as he would a dear loved one. As he had done so many times with Beth.

And in holding Ann in such a way, feeling the soft warmth of her flesh against his own, in knowing the nearness

85

without demanding of the body, an ache choked in his throat.

For much too long he had missed the true meaning of love.

There was magic in love, a magic that touched the soul as strongly as the body. And a person needed that touch far more than the physical expression of love.

Ann lay in his arms, as if wanting the same thing he did. As if hungering for this kind of affection and food. But he didn't really want to desire this form of need. He wanted to merely take a woman, think nothing other than what the pleasure of the body and the final act could sooth over his nerves. Possess her physically—nothing more.

Yet he didn't move to make any outward pass, no action to change the mood or the situation.

For a long time they lay in each other's arms in this manner, neither moving, neither doing more than breathing.

The rising and falling of Ann's breasts, like soft, warm supple cushions against his own chest, was part of the spark that finally changed inaction to action. Her skin was warm, hot against his.

The need had grown slowly, logically, as it should. When a man makes true love to a woman he wants her in every way more than any other woman on earth.

The drinks, the mood, the time, the place, the unsettled pathway of his life in the last years was probably to blame, he told himself, as his lips found the hollow of Ann's creamy white throat.

Her slender arms dragged him closer as a tremble moved the full length of her body. That was an action of a woman embracing her one and only man—her lover.

Yes, he thought, *she was captured by the same emotional need he felt.*

A thrill shot over him and his lips moved upwards, finding her full red lips.

She tensed, her hands covered the back of his neck, her mouth opened to his kiss and he felt those wonderful moist lips draw on his tongue as if they were greedily hungry.

He was painfully aware of the warmth of her body, the firmness of her thighs they pressed up to his, the hot de-

86

sire of her hips.

They were as two fused humans, locked in time, trapped by a greedy need that refused to let itself be released.

Breaking from the kiss, he heard Ann sob.

His own voice spoke.

"Oh, Ann...Ann...Ann."

It was the cry of a desperate agony building up in him. One that he could not control any more than he could control the beating of his heart.

"Ann...Ann..."

She seemed to surge closer, her body fitting beautifully against his own, as if they had been physically made for one another; as if all their lives had been lived for this moment when they would find each other.

It was a fantasy, but one he could not shatter—nor did he want to.

How they began, when their bodies took on a different kind of glow, new warmth that demanded, he was not quite sure. For in such an insanity that both were now experiencing, it was impossible to really know any actual order of events.

He was in a darkened world of sensation and feeling, emotion, where sight and sound, where reality fused into impressions, but had no order, for they became subordinate to the experience.

His body was aware of hers, moving. The softness, the warmth, the supple rhythm, shifting under him.

Sounds, hidden in pleasure, became shadows that accented the union of their bodies. It was like riding a wave, an emotional surfing through a storm coming at them from all directions at once. All sensation mated with total physical bonding, drowning all other awareness in its fusion of their two beings into one unified explosion of joyous energy. It was like some magnificent beginning, the instant of total love when the universe expanded into reality in the so-called Big Bang of Creation!

He heard his own voice crying out as he felt the tension of their forms surge together one last time draining out the ecstasy before oblivion could shatter awareness.

* * * * * * *

Ann felt a terrible loss, as she watched Joe's car disappear down Normandie Avenue away from the apartment that she still shared with Mari Thornton.

It was as if some part of herself were leaving, disappearing into the distance.

Something had happened the night before; something she had tried to reason out all the way home.

The drive had been a study in silence and their good-bye had been awkward, distant. Yet even in the silence and awkwardness, Ann was fully aware that what, in the beginning had been a cheap shack-up job for a chance into the door of fame, was now turning into something more binding; and it shouldn't. That was a no-no, which reasonable minds would refuse to even consider. Love had nothing to do with her moves in connecting with this lovely wonderful man. It was insanity. It was something some teenager might experience in a mad crush for the first boy who had awkwardly kissed her at the doorstep of her parent's home. Not something an experienced woman, like herself, had the right to fall victim to. Pure, wonderful, lovely, fantastic madness.

How could that fit into her plans to become an actor, to make a name in films, to become a Star?

Hardly at all. Never. No place. It was not part of her living jigsaw. It shattered all the other pieces to the floor, leaving no room for anything else on the table of her living experience.

Unless she pushed it away and picked up the scattered pieces of her more realistic dream.

Turning, she looked up at the sun, blinded for a moment, thinking about how a new day could mean so much.

Oh, how perfect life was. In his arms it had been beyond wonderful. It had been everything that life was meant to be. And all illusion.

They didn't even know one another. All they really knew was how fantastic the sex was. And that was far beyond anything she had ever experienced with a man or woman. But sex was not love. Love was far more complex and required time to mature, to ferment into the fine, delicious, lasting wine necessary to survive years of tumbling marriage, years of struggling life, years of hell and damnation that the world shattered around all of those who lived in it.

Annoyed by the thought, Ann went up to the apartment, took out her key and opened the door.

The place was quite, dark.

As she made her way toward the bedroom, a voice called out.

"That you?"

Ann continued to the door of her bedroom, ignoring the call.

She was entering her room when Mari suddenly appeared.

"Hello," the other woman said, following Ann into the bedroom.

"Hello," Ann said, tiredly.

"I missed you, how'd things go?" The question was more automatic, as if the woman had felt it necessary to say something like that. Something polite and as an opening statement to some destination only she understood.

"Fine."

"I bet!" was the bitter reply. "I just bet it was!"

"What's wrong with you?" Ann demanded, glaring at Mari. All she wanted was to be alone, not get into some kind of vicious battle with this woman.

There was a strange, angry expression in Mari's eyes. It was the expression of a person obsessed with jealousy and torment.

Mari finally said: "I...can't...go on like this!"

Ann said nothing, instead sat down on her bed, looked up at the other woman as if saying, won't you please go to hell. But no bitter words came from her lips. She felt more sorry for Mari than hate. And, anyway, it would be difficult to feel hate for anyone right now. Her whole heart was brimming with thrilling excitement over her feeling for Joe—even while mentally wanted to fight the emotion.

And she certainly didn't want to get into some kind of conflict that would shatter the lovely mood that had enveloped her in his arms. She could still feel him inside her like some real thing, all memory all lovely memory she wanted to keep captured within her being.

"I've been up all night," Mari said, still standing in front of the door. She was dressed in a filmy nightgown that showed off her big breasts, the nipples hard against the cloth. "All I could think of was what was happening...to us. The other night! It's not right that—"

Her voice was choked with anguish. The woman's eyes pleaded with Ann to say something.

"Mari...please! I don't want to talk about it right now!"

"I *have* to talk about it. I'm going out of my mind. It's hard enough being in the same apartment with you, knowing you are so close. And wanting you. The least you can do is let me make love to you—that wouldn't hurt you. And it would help me so much!"

Mari moved toward the bed, her eyes focused on Ann's body, as if greedily attempting to caress it.

"Please, Mari! I don't want to...hurt you!" Ann exploded, standing. "Call it quits! Stop right now! No further. Never!"

Mari stopped. The expression on her face hardened, the look in her eyes fired almost insanely.

Then suddenly she leaped forward.

The attack was so fast that Ann couldn't defend herself at first.

The other woman's hand slapped out, hitting Ann's face, while at the same time her body pushed Ann backwards against the bed.

Stunned, not able to believe what was happening, because of its suddenness, Ann lay there, helpless under the weight of the other woman.

A hand touched her skirt, pulled upwards and she heard the ripping of cloth. Fingers clutched her thigh, biting hard lips attempted to find hers.

Ann struggled, fighting to get the weight of the other woman off her body.

The advantage was Mari's.

It was like fighting five people at once.

Both surprise and fear mixed to make Ann weak.

Terror, not at what Mari could do to her, but the unexpected, insanity of the attack caused her own actions to be seemingly useless, struck out aimlessly, in panic.

Then something happened. What, exactly, Ann didn't know. Possibly it was because Mari had managed to place open moist lips on hers, momentarily side-tracking the woman's attention. In any case the balance of weight changed just slightly. But it was enough.

Ann surged upwards with all her strength, then twisted, shoving the other woman from her.

Frantically she attempted to leap from the bed, but Mari jumped after her, tackling Ann like a football player, throwing her forward.

Ann's head hit the floor and for a dazed moment blackness was fluttering over her.

She struggled out of the dark black pool that had threatened consciousness.

Mari was on top of her again, gasping, a tangled heap of legs, arms, and hands, moving over her body like something erotically insane beasts from some horror film.

Fear choked at Ann and she moved, kicking with her knee. Violently, desperately fighting.

The aim was perfect and other woman jerked back as if having been pulled by puppet strings. She fell backwards, her head hitting into the bed, hands covering the pit of her stomach.

Ann gathered herself to her feet, stared down at the other, agonized woman, feeling both pity and disgust.

After some time, Mari caught her breath, and laying there, her eyes turned up to Ann's.

A nasty sneer curled Mari's lips.

"You…dirty…little…tramp!...Slut!" the woman gasped in agony. It was some time before she could continue, but after catching her breath, recovering, while silence answer her verbal assault, she screamed: "Damned slut! What right do you have to stand there and act like little Annie prude? You're a tramp—and worse! You play at teasing people! At least I'm willing to admit what I am. I want you—that's all. You teased, played at it—I hate your damned guts!"

91

With that last outburst, Mari stood, started threateningly toward Ann.

"Don't!" Ann yelled, both fear and fury choking at her.

Mari leaped, this time her hands reached out for Ann's throat. The face that stared into hers was that of pure insane hatred.

Ann had never seen such a thing.

Automatic instinct saved her from those clawing hands that would wrap around her throat if given a chance.

She pushed the arms to one side, then clawed out a right across Mari's face.

Her nails drew a red-blood line on the woman's right cheek.

Then as Mari turned for another attack, Ann doubled up her fist and swung. She had never hit another human being with her fist and really didn't know what she was doing. Instinct, fear, and most of all disgust at what was happening controlled her actions.

The aim was better than she could have expected. Her fist hit Mari in the jaw and the woman snapped backwards, shock whitening her face.

Ann followed through with her attack, knowing that the only way to stop what was happening was to over-power the other woman.

The two of them tangled, fell on the bed, but with Ann on top.

The weight of her body on the other woman gave the advantage necessary to lock Mari's arms against the bed.

For a long time the woman struggled, frantically attempting to get free, but Ann had placed herself so that it was impossible for Mari to do anything other than lay there helpless.

When the woman had exhausted herself, Ann said. "Okay, are you through?"

"Damn you slut!" Mari screamed.

Ann hit the woman across the face, the anger of what had been said before burning the hatred into live action. She felt no sorrow, but a sense of guilt. Being cruel had always been a hateful thing with Ann. Sure, there had been many

92

times in the past when she had done damned cruel things. And the fact that what Mari had said was partly true, hurt Ann.

After a long time, still breathing heavily, Mari finally looked up, her eyes more calm, her features more relaxed.

"Get off me, I don't want you to touch me!" The hatred was still there, but not the violent insanity.

Ann slowly moved from the other woman, careful for any surprise or unexpected attack.

But Mari lay there, still breathing hard, but saying nothing.

It was then that a decision had to be made. Instantly. She had to move out. Right away. Right into a motel, if necessary.

Ann was beginning to pack her things, ready to leave the apartment for good before Mari moved or said anything.

The voice was regretful, but still filled with anguish and a touch of hate.

"I guess it's better you leave," Mari observed coldly. Then a little later added: "I'm not sorry—only that I let my temper get the best of me!"

"Who cares!" Ann snapped, her own anger still seething through her.

"I do." Mari was sitting on the bed, looking at Ann, and there was just the hint of regret on her features. "I'm sorry, Ann."

She ignored the woman.

Some fifteen minutes later, when she was starting to carry her suitcase into the living room, Mari suddenly lifted from the bed, rushed over to her, throwing demanding arms around her neck.

"Please, please forgive me...I love you...I want you and I don't care what it—"

"Stop!" Ann said in a threatening voice.

Mari froze, pulled back and for a moment it looked as if the woman was about to attack her again, then she finally relaxed. But there was a terrible look of hatred in the woman's eyes.

A chill rushed over Ann. That hate was a violent, dangerous hate.

"Please, can't we just forget the mistake?" Ann finally said. "It was wrong from the beginning. You and me like that. I'm sorry, but that's the way things are!"

She almost added that something had truly happened to her, something that had changed her outlook on life. She would never want another woman. That side of her was dead. Maybe she had grown up a little; maybe it was only a natural part of maturity. They said that homosexual relations were merely immature relations. Most people went through a homosexual stage and grew out of it in their teens. Maybe that was psychobabble, but it might have some truth for many people. Certainly for her, it was a factor, no doubt. She had outgrown that curiosity—which had been shallow to begin with.

Her own mistake had been not realizing what she really wanted in life. Up to this point she had lived for kicks. But there was surely more in life than kicks.

What that might be for her, Ann wasn't quite sure.

Possibly a career; possibly something else.

She would have to find out.

Turning, going to the phone, Ann said to the woman:

"I'm sorry, Mari, this is really all my fault— but...then I fooled myself more than I fooled you."

She picked up the receiver and started to dial, as Mari's bedroom door slammed shut.

Ann heard sobbing in the other room as she ordered a taxicab.

As she hung up the phone she felt a terrible sense of confusion. Her heart went out to Mari, who was sobbing in the background, a muffled, anguished sound. But that couldn't be helped.

Where now? What next?

There was Joe Dickenson. But how long could that last? What, after that?

Sighing, she took a pack of cigarettes from her purse, lighted one and tried to ignore the sobbing from Mari's room.

CHAPTER TEN

Walter Bennick stared across the desk like a furious mountain of rage, his features thick and crimson. Over and over again his fist was pounding on the desktop, while his eyes burned into Joe Dickenson's.

"I don't care *why, why, why* you weren't bending over backwards with Carol last night—I don't care for any reasons or any excuses! No matter how important or personal your engagement might have been. I told you that I don't give a damned how you did it, but that Carol was supposed to be on the lot at six in the morning sharp!" The man's voice was tense, but hadn't really raised above a whisper—a controlled, dangerous whisper.

Slowly the large man stood, his eyes never leaving Joe's.

A shiver shook through Joe. The first thing that had hit him that morning, upon arriving at work was a demand to report to the Studio Boss' office immediately. The first statement to come from the man was:

"Where's Carol...?" The conversation which followed had been brief and to the point. Joe had explained that he thought everything was all right. That he had talked to Carol and told her that something personal, very important had come up the night before. That's when Walter Bennick started pounding his desk.

For a long time the other man glared at him, and it wasn't hard to imagine the guy leaping over the desk and lunging at his throat. In fact, Joe braced himself instinctively for any attack, verbal or physical that might come, as surely it must. But suddenly Walter Bennick's features slowly began relaxing. He pulled a cigar from his coat pocket, lighted,

95

but never did those fierce eyes leave Joe's.

"Look, son, I want you to know something. Maybe you don't realize the full importance of the assignment I gave you. I'm not the lug-headed fool one might think. I have a temper, sure, but I also have a brain—and a heart, if you will." Walter Bennick's voice was soft, controlling himself or being sarcastic.

"Mr. Dickenson, you have a head on your shoulders. Surely you know what kind of a slut that woman is! You know what kind of things she wants. Well, you should know what we want from her, too. I really don't care how you get results—I thought I had made that quite clear at the beginning." His cigar struck out at the air, to accent some of his points, the light in his eyes seemed to darken the longer he talked. It was as if he were working himself up to a point—and a pitch.

Joe tensed, shifting nervously in the chair he was seated in.

"Now that tramp wants something from you. I don't care if it is reasonable or not. I'm not interested! The only thing I care about is getting this damned movie finished—and without any headaches." The man was breathing heavily now, and he sat down, glared at Joe.

"Carol, like some other women in this business is a very frustrated person. She has gone through life giving a lot of herself to the Industry. Oh, I know I've been against her—on a basic...well, business...level—from the beginning. Because I saw where it might lead. But...you were the one who put her down our throats with a big sales talk. Saying it would make a B picture into a first run one without any extra budget—since Carol was having a hard time finding work, just because of her being late. Being a problem. Just being...her.

"Now—I've made it clear about my feelings about her—and your role in the matter. You know what I expect. Now tell me," he said, shouting, "why the Hell you weren't loving Carol to Hell and back last night? What's wrong with you? Every man in the universe wants to bang her body. I've been told she's a super slut in heat, no holds barred. So...what's with you? Don't you like women?"

96

Stunned, Joe started to say something then realized that there really wasn't anything to say. Up to being called into the office, he had been sure everything was all right. But, that had been a big mistake. He had underestimated Carol—and her demands on him. But he also thought she understood him and was, at least, humanly considerate.

"That sexpot wants you—and wants you to play all kinds of games with her! She so much as said so this morning when I called, wondering where she was, that there just wasn't any chance of her being on the lot today. *She* told me where to get off! She told me to stuff it right up the dark side of my backend, and shove it deep, was her added demand before hanging up."

The man was leaning forward, a huge monster of anger towering over Joe.

"Damn it man, nobody tells me where to get off! If it weren't for this picture, and the money invested, I'd junk her good." An oily grin passed over the man's face, but it held no emotion.

"Joe—you go over there and give the girl what she wants—and get her here as soon as possible. I'm not going to hold up production any longer. Either she does come here before afternoon shooting, in time to go to work, *or you both are finished!*"

The last was fairly screamed at Joe.

"Now get the hell out to here! I don't want to see you in this studio again—until Carol Clements walks on this lot! And I'm telling the gate guard to not let you in unless you have the CC ticket with you! Got me?"

With that, Walter Bennick turned and went to his seat, ignoring Joe.

For a moment Joe sat there, trying hard to think of something to say. Then he realized there was nothing to say. Walter Bennick's word was law, and final. As of that moment he was fired unless Carol Clements walked on the lot before twelve that afternoon.

Sick, a grinding sensation cutting at his stomach like a million knives, Joe stood and quickly left the office.

All the way to Carol Clements house, Joe Dickenson was cursing himself and cursing Ann Farrow. Of all the fool things he could have done was play games with a nobody instead of completely bending to Carol's will. He should have known better.

But he had known better, and something had driven him toward Ann, and frantically away from Carol.

The rage burned so violently that when he finally arrived at Carol's house, he sat there in the car, smoking one cigarette after another, trying to calm his nerves so that it would be possible to face the woman. Every nerve screamed to go in there and beat the hell out of her. And he'd never hit a woman.

The rage subsided, slowly. Logically he realized that Bennick had to be bluffing. He could hardly dump the picture at this point. The man had already backed down on his original threat to dump CC and him if the woman ever missed being on the set every morning.

Still, even then, his job was on the line, ultimately. If he couldn't pull this picture in under schedule, with CC he would find himself looking for another job—and maybe not in Hollywood. Bennick was quite able to make life hell in the town for anybody he happened to dislike. The man had a reputation of ruining people's careers as well as making them. It was a dangerously sharp double-edged sword the man could carelessly swing. It was all part of the game. And if one wanted to succeed in the business they had to play to win.

The trouble with him was that he really wasn't sure what he wanted out of life. Oh, success. But his personal life had become tragically twisted. Even then he'd been amazingly lucky. Things had seemed nearly effortless.

Everything had moved fairly easily for him all his life, until the difficulty with Beth. But that had smoothed over, finally. He had accepted the situation of where he would be going in the world. He had tried to do the best job possible at work, hoping someday to climb his way up to production. But, he realized, sitting there, everything had come automatically, like each step in a staircase came automatically after the other. Everything had fallen into place, without any real driving effort. Life had been fairly uncomplicated. Work, women, and high living. What a dream.

The first temptation was to rush into Carol's house and raise hell with her, like Bennick had done with him. But then, he realized that would be like throwing fire on fire. Carol wouldn't allow a man to tell her where to get off. The fact was that he had let himself become a male prostitute at her demand. He'd been stupid denying that point. No matter how much he fought the idea, he was nothing but a stud, putting out for the lady who had something he wanted. She had played hardball with him and had all the balls in her corner. This was made quite clear by the fact that she hadn't shown up for work that day.

What CC wanted CC got. Or else!

Sighing, Joe slipped out of the car, started up the walkway to the large front porch.

After ringing the doorbell and waiting for several moments, Joe heard footsteps approaching the door and felt a sense of inner defeat. He thought about his life, and about Ann Farrow and the strangely wonderful evening they had enjoyed the night before.

A special experience which this immediate one was destined to pervert.

He wondered if it had been worth it

Then the door opened and the maid stood there, smiling.

"Miss Clements is expecting you, Mr. Dickenson," she announced politely.

Joe followed the young woman into the house.

"She's in the playroom," the maid said. There was a smirk on her lips, and her tone of voice underscored the last word.

"Thanks," he said, politely, but not with an edge of bitterness.

She grinned, said: "Well, I do believe, Mr. D, that our Missy is a very playful lady."

Joe gave the woman a double take, surprised.

The maid simply shrugged knowingly, and actually, for a moment looked sympathetically at him.

Taking his time, Joe started for the playroom, across the living room and then hesitated before the closed door, behind which Carol Clements would be awaiting his arrival.

He lighted a cigarette and took a deep drag, telling his nerves to keep calm. The fact was that he had played unfair with Carol, according to the rules, which the two of them had agreed upon. She would be a good little girl as long as he did what she told him; otherwise it could be serious trouble.

Technically he'd broken their verbal contract. She'd kept her side of the bargain. Hate it or not, he had "signed on" to her demands and she had kept her promises as long as he did his duty and played love-stud at her demand.

Now, easily, Carol could ruin his career at Bennick Studios. All she had to do was tell him to go to hell. The picture would be finished; the studio would find ways to get her to the set—even if it cost them a lot of money. But in the end they would make money on the film. But he would be out of a job, and it wouldn't be so easy to get another one.

Carol Clements held all the cards and he didn't dare let her know just how powerful her position was.

Finally he opened the door, stepped into the playroom.

"Well, hello," came a pleasant voice. "Close the door, will you, darlin'?"

The door had no more closed than suddenly Carol, who had been sitting at the bar, turned and threw a glass at him.

The aim, luckily was bad—possibly she had intended on missing.

The glass smashed into the door behind him, shattering.

"Hell, damn you!" she screamed, standing.

"What's wrong?" he asked, puzzled. "For Christ sake, Carol—"

"You know damned well," Carol said in a tight voice. "You copped out on me last night. That wasn't part of the bargain!"

"Carol, I'm sorry—I couldn't help it."

"To hell you couldn't help it!" she cried, furious.

Joe took a step forward, tried to smile, said: "Carol, now what's really wrong? You're a nice, reasonable woman...surely you...have to understand we all have a private life—one which involves others. Be reasonable."

"Screw you!" she snapped. "Pardon the implication!"

"Come on—can't we be realistic about all this? The film is business. We're all professionals. Now what's wrong?"

"You!"

"I told you I was sorry." He felt sick inside, because regardless of how it sounded, he was begging for forgiveness.

A strange expression clouded Carol's face. She relaxed suddenly.

"What was so important that you couldn't be with me last night?"

"Personal!"

"Nothing is personal between people like us!" she snapped, but the tone of her voice was softer.

"I'm sorry. It was *too* personal. It has nothing to do with you—and—"

"I don't want your excuses!" Carol announced. "I want my big ...lover with me...that's all.

"Come here!"

The command rankled him, but there was nothing he could do but be submissive.

Slowly he stepped forward, and only when he had come within a yard of the woman did he stop.

She was dressed in a tight blue blouse, which accented the lush shape of her lush breasts. Stretch pants showed off the rest of her body in a raw sexual way.

She was a female tigress, dressed to feast on her lover—at least in a sexual emotional way. That was one thing about Carol that Joe had learned, fast. Once she wanted something, she would go all out to get it. First afternoon she had been direct about what she wanted, and the rules of her game had started then—loud and clear.

Carol moved her right hand to the top of the blouse, meaningfully undid one button, then her fingers edged downwards to the second, which flicked away expertly; on the third she hesitated only long enough to make the action fully effective. The third button unlatched itself and the large opening that fell loose around her breasts exposed the fact she was wearing nothing on under the blouse.

"I have a hungry body, Joe. My titties hurt. And you did a dirty trick on me. You know the deal—and I just couldn't do anything else but make it very, very clear to you that my appearing at work on time each morning is *only* because you have continued to please me. The minute you stop pleasing me, Joe, then, you see what happens." She stepped closer and her lush breasts pressed against his chest. "I don't like it when my lover-baby isn't around. Believe me, you aren't the only man—but I like my men one at a time. One sex slave is enough to soothe my aching body. I want you...in me...on me...around me...I need what you have down there..."

She wiggled voluptuously against him. "I'm hoary hot for a hard...tricky dicky. And I want yours. All of it. Big and hot and meaty...just throbbing in me."

Her arms slipped around his neck, and he felt her hot breath on his face, then smelled the reek of. Liquor. The glazed expression in her eyes was now obvious: raw, naked, lust.

Impulse made him want to push her away. There was something filthy and disgusting about the set-up, about Carol Clements. What in the world did she think she was? What made her believe it was possible to play independent with the Studio?

"I know what you're thinking, Dicky boy!" she murmured.

"I doubt it," he snapped back, voice thick with emotion.

"Oh, You'd like to kick my ass, you would. I can see it all over your face. You're so damned pissed at me that...if I didn't want you so bad you'd probably rape me in vicious fury! Oh, that's a thought, now, isn't it?"

She laughed. "I just love it when a man is all fury and passion and so bloated with all that...anger. Makes me wild just thinking what you wanna do—what you're going to do to me."

She ran her lips against his cheek, then let them linger almost touching his. "I bet you'd like to stick me deep..."

102

The woman's body surged against him, wantonly. "I'd like that. Just take me like a savage animal, ravish me, I don't care. You can't be wild enough…I want to be ravished by a beast. I want to feel all that fury entering my body, ramming at me. I want you furiously hard mad. Brutal. Just do it!"

She stepped back slightly, took his hand, put it against her breast. "Suck 'em, hard, love. Rip my clothes off. Take that, Dicky…" and she reached between his legs with an open palm, brazenly exploring. "Get it out and make it mine! That entire big lovely male hard thing! I want it, bad!"

It was impossible to believe her words. She'd not come on like this before. And the raging anger shifted into furious passion.

She literally crushed herself against him.

The anger, the frustration, the pure insanity of what his life was becoming—had become—and most of all, this bitch forcing herself on him, was just too much to deal with all at once.

His arms crushed Carol brutally against him, as his mouth covered hers, open. Savagely he thrust his tongue deep into her mouth, as if almost wishing to choke her with it.

A convulsive shudder shook the woman, and her hips surged to his, moving like they were possessed of a will of their own.

One thought was beating like drums in his brain:

He'd screw the goddamned hell out of this bitching whore. When he was finished with her she would know just what kind of man he was, just what kind of lion she had tangled with; and if he did it right, Carol Clements would have experienced something she would never forget in all her life.

It was going to be a union of hate, a union of brutal, cruel passion.

Joe had never experienced anything so violent and over-powering as the exchange of physical blows which their bodies rained upon each other. It was not giving, it wasn't even taking—more like two animals attempting to actually hurt each other.

Sequence of events were scattered, a blur.

He felt the agonizing clawing of Carol's nails as they ripped at his shirt, fairly pulling it away from his body.

To him, this was not a woman, but a combatant, a being whom he had to overwhelm—not conquer, for that had already been done the first day—if the term could be used in the case of Carol Clements.

His hands were already beginning to tear at the blouse, and he felt the material starting to strain and then rip under his fingers. One hand found the back of her head, the fingers tangled with the short hairs there and twisted, tightening until Carol broke away from his bruising kiss, a low gasp of pain uttering from her lips.

Her fingers tore, brutally at his pants buckle, with no concern to anything other than ripping him naked.

Like a savage, Joe grabbed her hands, then shoved her across the room, toward the sofa.

Joe rushed after her, and his body came down hard, against the tangle of female flesh that twisting wildly under his, entangling around him like a multi-armed snake. A gasp sounded from Carol's throat as she fell backwards against the large sofa.

Her dress was torn from her body, and the bra was stripped away from one hefty breast that pointed at him like a red eye. Carol laughed excitedly, and attempted to embrace him with her arms.

One look into her eyes told him that she knew what kind of game he was going to play, and the light there assured him that it suited her just fine—maybe too damned much.

But it was too late to stop now, for the emotion was already bursting out of him.

Her fingers were already clawing at his zipper.

"Give it...hurry..."

She was overwhelming. There was no way to avoid totally responding.

Suddenly the two of them locked together, and this time it was a two-way battle.

Like a wild creature from some hellish dimension, he suddenly leaped at her and she totally encased him in her arms. Those lips parted, wide and covered his, almost sobbing.

Everything happened so fast that he could hardly believe it. They were tangled together, then suddenly she was arching up against him, stark naked. Only then did he realize he was just as naked and her thighs parted wide. She grabbed at him and he suddenly deeply embedded her hungry body. The woman moaned in her anguished joy at having him so deeply captured.

He was aware of the shear voluptuous pleasure of her gripping firmly around him, her whole body embracing his as they raged against one another.

And at the same time he was insanely angry at how easily she had driven him to this point. All he wanted to do was attack her like some hateful creature he needed to demolish. His body rammed again and again at her and she moaned and gasped, then sobbed in her ecstatic joy.

His own body kept slamming at her, responding to the voluptuous pleasure ripping through him. It was a brutal taking, without any tenderness, caring, nothing but pure animal energy.

It was like being in a hot trap from which there was no escape.

Then suddenly the two of them cried out almost. At that point all he became aware of was the sensations raging through him. He was riding on a wild beast of electric pleasure that ravished every nerve and muscle. Reality simply exploded away.

PARLEY IN PASSION, BY CHARLES NUETZEL

CHAPTER ELEVEN

How long he lay there, literally in her arms, in a half-world, he didn't know. Slowly reality came back into focus.

He was aware of her lips on him, greedily ravishing what she had just so totally possessed. She moaned in her joy as he found himself responding to her skillful lovemaking.

And hating it. While loving it.

God she was good! He realized they were stretched out on the floor, the lush rug softly cushioning his back as she orally feasted on him.

He was being lifted up on wave after wave of tingling pleasure. Then suddenly she lifted away, straddling his hips, turned and then placing her hands under her large breasts, said: "Suck 'em, love!"

As she spoke, her hips had lifted and moved, shifted and then surged down, once again totally enveloping him in her.

"Suck me, please, darling," she moaned, leaning over so that her nipples were just above his mouth. "Suck me real hard!"

If Carol Clements was making demands on him, it was his own fault. And, in a way, most Casting Directors made the same demand on many young starlets. Either the girl gave out, on command or she didn't get even a chance at walking into the door of Fame.

Everybody was a slave to somebody else. The powerful used and abused those under them.

He had used his power to seduce women hungry to get their big break and thought he was it. That game was cruel. And that's what CC was playing with him.

And he hated her and himself and the whole situation.

Joe realized more fully than ever before that the life he had been living in the past years was a useless exercise in escape, without any meaning.

He felt her hips moving and then her breast was crushed against his mouth.

After that he didn't care any more. He was thinking about nothing but the angry fury of his body, her body, the demanding heat that totally burned out any other thoughts.

The strange thing was that most men would think this was an ideal set-up. A lush, hot, passionate woman, internationally known, commanding him to make love to her, to bend to her will. Her hot demands.

He was aware of her moving very slowly up and down on him and aware of her breasts taking turns in smothering against his mouth. She shivered in total joy at what was happening and started moving even slower, lingeringly, literally savoring the feast she was making of him.

His mind blurred and after that everything was sensation. His thoughts were lost in the fiery depths of her body that continued to possess him completely.

Then a suddenly scream of shear joy sounded from the women, cutting through his thoughts and focusing them on what she was doing. Her body had suddenly arched against him, her whole frame going rigid then all at once her hips were furiously ramming against his as she sobbed in anguished ecstasy.

Then the anger raged up inside him. The orgasms were completed and he still felt a fury of how she had used him, demanded his body, crushed his will to her overwhelming seduction.

He felt cheap, disgusted with himself.

And suddenly he wanted nothing more than to hit her, smash her lovely, beautiful, cruelly demanding face.

Sick inside, totally reacting, not even realizing what was happening, Joe found his right hand striking out, instinctively, without thought to what he was doing, hitting Carol across the cheek.

The woman's face blanched and then a glassy expression took shape in her eyes and a tremble rushed over

108

her.

She clawed out at his face with curled fingers.

His left hand blocked the attack, and then, slowly he forced Carol's arms down against the floor, and pinned them under her knees.

"Love you...love you..." she gasped, wiggling wantonly. "Love you. You little shit!"

Her breasts were heaving, her lips parted, gasping in air, her eyes were hot fires looking up into his in open pleasure. She was enjoying the attack, the violence.

Angrily, not able to control the surging fury bursting through him, Joe hit her face again and she sobbed in excitement.

A disgusted stab shot through Joe as he realized this was exactly what Carol wanted. She literally wanted him to hit her again and wanted to fight back.

Something cold and terribly sick shuddered through Joe. He had heard about women wanting to be hit and he had heard of men who got their kicks hitting women around. But never before in his life had he done such a thing nor known a woman who wanted him to.

"Don't stop, you shit!" she fairly screamed. "Oh, don't stop. I love you...oh, love it!"

Strangely the impulse to hit her again and again built up in him like some insane desire to beat her to a whimpering mass of flesh pleading for him to stop.

But his hand didn't move.

Instead he started to lift from her body, wanting to end this charade now—before it went any further.

He had no more than released his weight from her arms than Carol was at him, her hands striking out at his face, her body surging up to find his. Those clawing fingers found the back of his neck and dug in deep, holding him so that her lips could have his all to themselves.

Their bodies embraced there on the sofa, his arms fully pinning her legs down, her form writhing, excited to a pitch, which slowly had its effect on his own body. It was impossible to escape the bold, voluptuous excitement that her form was generating. In fact, no man would find it possible to ignore the sensual power of her deep, searching tongue, her hot, damp breasts pressing against his chest, her clawing, hurting fingernails against his neck.

A curse broke from his lips as the kiss broke.

Angrily, Joe shoved her back and suddenly their bodies were surging together, violently attacking each other.

He felt sick with every instant of pleasure that her love-making was demanding him to feel.

Joe wanted to stop, wanted to kill her, wanted so many things other than the perverse relationship that was now taking place.

She was a wild, wonderful, wanton woman, without limits, and driving at him at full force. She hands, lips, body wouldn't stop hungrily stroking, kissing, writhing against his flesh; thrilling, pawing his hard muscles with her intense need.

He was a helpless slave to the female sex machine that was now in command of his nerves. It was as if he were chained down against her, forced to respond from an outside power, moved through the erotic actions of physical union, against his will.

Then thought, awareness, reality, sliced away and all the sensations of their final explosive ecstatic bodies strained and then finally they fell away from one another.

Sick, his stomach churning, his mind revolting, body sweating from every pore, Joe lifted away from Carol Clements, stood, turned, too disgusted to look at her.

She was still gasping in deep, uncontrolled gulps of breath as he started getting his clothing together.

As he put his jacket on, over the shredded remains of his shirt, Carol sat up, said:

"Oh, God, Joe...you don't know what that did to me. You were *great!*"

Controlling the sickness, the grinding anguish and anger that threatened to expose his true feelings, Joe said:

"You'll report to the studio?"

Carol was silent for a moment and then told him "If that's what you want. But you be here when I get back—understand?"

"Have a heart!" Joe heard his own, pleading voice cry out.

110

A throaty laugh mocked him. "Why should I?"

Disgusted, Joe went to the bar, poured himself a drink as Carol started out of the room.

"I'll get dressed," she told him, closing the door behind her.

Shaking, Joe gulped the whiskey, and wondered if all this was worth the reward.

Sure, it had been sexually exciting. But no man who cared about himself, or about women, in general, could enjoy a sexual attack, without hating himself.

Carol was sick. Damned sick. Too damned sick.

Joe poured himself another strong scotch and looked at the glass, realizing that he had an uncontrollable urge to get really drunk, and stay soused for a long, long time.

How the hell had he gotten himself into such a situation? And where was it going to end? Carol might never want to get him out of her clutches; and that could be just too bad for him, and the career. If she decided she wanted him, and was willing to be a good girl, what could he do? She would become the Star of the studio, and everything would revolve around her.

Of course, he could start all over, somewhere else. He knew a lot of people in Hollywood. But what if Bennick wanted to Blackball him?

Things were getting thick, and he couldn't see his way out of them.

As he gulped the second scotch down, shivering from reaction, the image of a beautiful blonde haired, green-eyed woman came into his mind.

Ann. Farrow...

If only she were here, right now, he thought, almost desperately. It was pretty good between them. They were two, good, healthy animals, but there was more to it than that. He felt relaxed and good with her and he felt something else, which wasn't as easy to define.

Just then Carol returned smiling, looking quite childlike in that voluptuous sexy way that had become famous on the screen.

"Hello, Darling," she cooed, stepping up beside him. Her lips touched his cheek, very possessively. "I like you too much. We are a good thing, you and me," she observed, taking a sip from his drink. "You are just too, too much."

A chuckle shook her breasts, which were half exposed behind the low cut neckline of the tight fitting blue dress.

Joe fought his anger and realized that the only way he could continue to play down the middle, like he had been doing, was act out the part she wanted him to play.

The fact that he was willing to act this part and could force himself to do so, now, was almost morally shattering. But his job was to please Carol Clements. Violent emotions had battled themselves out in the sex-fight a little while before—but not completely out for him. And a new element had developed: a terrible and complete disgust for Carol Clements and what she stood for.

But, he said "Sorry about what happened."

She laughed, patted his cheek. "Why be sorry? It was great. If only that kind of thing could happen to a girl all the time."

She shrugged, her eyes bright, blazing: "But...of course, that happened by accident—but now, who knows? Maybe it could happen by design sometime." Then as if by afterthought she kissed his lips, almost tenderly. "You know, I didn't realize how much fun that could be. You really gave me a lot to think about, Joe. A very, very lot."

Carol teased him with her breasts against his chest, her hips against his, then a soft hand caressed the back of his neck.

"You're a beast!" she accused, her right hand clawing at the back of his neck, the fingernails digging deep.

Automatically, Joe grabbed her right arm, twisted it away from him. He was on the verge of breaking it when he heard her laughter.

"See, Joe. Such things *could* be arranged!" she observed, pulling free from his grasp. "You're so easy to make mad. Oh, delicious man! And you're so strong and...oh so hard! I'll feel you all day inside me."

With that she turned and literally left the room.

"Be here later...for me!" she called. "Dinner and sex!"

112

CHAPTER TWELVE

When Joe Dickenson arrived at his office that afternoon, at three, his secretary looked up from her desk, said "There's been several phone calls for you." Then she handed him a piece of paper with several names.

Glancing over the list he spotted his ex-wife's name and Ann Farrow's.

"What did Beth want?" he inquired.

"She wouldn't say. When I told her you weren't in, she said she would get hold of you, but she sounded, well—"

"Anxious?"

June smiled. "Yes."

Joe went into his own office, sat down, picked up the phone, and dialed Ann Farrow's number before he realized that she wouldn't be home during the day.

He looked at the list; his eyes hesitated at Beth's name.

Picking up the receiver again, he dialed his old home number. There was a long wait while the number rang half a dozen times. Then he hung up.

During the next few hours he took care of the rest of the calls, some to agents putting on the pressure for their clients and others directly from young starlet's who were making no bones about offering a good night out on the town— or in their bedrooms. Each offer meant the same thing: the casting couch.

"What's new, Darling?" would be the typical question. "Thought we might get together. How about dinner at my place?" That had been the offer from a redhead whom he had met some time before.

As he came to the end of the list there was Mari

Thornton's name on it.

Wondering what Mari wanted, Joe dialed, waited. When Mari's voice answered the phone, he identified himself.

"Oh, hello, Joe, how are things?"

"Fine as can be expected," he said distantly.

"I was wondering if we could get together?" she said in an anxious voice.

"Sorry, I'm terribly busy, right now."

There was a harsh edge to her voice when she said:

"But this is *very* important, Joe. I think you would like to know about it."

"About what?"

"I can't talk about it over the phone—but...it's about Ann Farrow." There was an element of intrigue in her voice.

An alarm bell rang in his brain. What could have happened to Ann?

"What's wrong?"

"Oh, nothing—but...well, it is pretty terrible. She moved out—we had a fight and—I thought you should know what happened—and *why* she moved." Emotion fired the last words.

Joe was silent for a long moment and then said: "I can't—today."

"Tonight?" Mari offered. "We could have dinner and..." the invitation was more implication than anything. Like too many other young actresses, Mari was putting in a plug for herself, with her body. She'd plug him in and give him a charge, a sampling of what was in the offering for a part in some film. The standard casting couch routine. She was lovely enough, and willing enough, but nothing had really been sparkling with Mari. It was as if she were going through the motions. Oh, her body twitched, and correct sounds came from her lips, and she knew everything there was to know in order to give a man what he wanted. But more like a prostitute going through her routine; nothing more. Not that many of them weren't just that standardized. Only Mari had some distance, some kind of patterned routine that was somewhat cool, even cold. As if she really didn't care all that much—perhaps she didn't. The woman didn't

114

matter to him one way or the other. There were too many like her. Plus she had plenty of connections that were more willing to service her acting needs. He had nothing against her as a person—and wasn't interested in getting himself that close. They were professional "friends" and not much more.

"Sorry—but, it's impossible! Not tonight!"

"When, then? I know you'll be glad that you found out about Ann." Again that intriguing suggestion of something off-color.

A shudder ticked his spine.

"Tomorrow afternoon, then," he suggested.

"That's fine."

"Oh, do you know where I could get hold of Ann?" he inquired.

"Are you kidding?" was the snapping reply.

"Okay, tomorrow—around noon."

He hung up, sat there wondering what the hell could have happened to cause Ann to move out. Or was she kicked out? There was that element in Mari's voice and something more. Something very dramatically wrong.

* * * * * * *

For Ann Farrow the day had been one of confusion and sheer madness. She had stayed in a hotel after leaving Mari Thornton, then gone to work the next day, foolishly, because that didn't give her any time to look for an apartment. That evening after work, she had started searching, by foot, a tiresome activity that left her discouraged and exhausted. When she reported to the hotel where she was still staying, Ann felt foot sore and worn out. She went to the hotel clerk and said: "Could you tell me where I could go to get an apartment—one bedroom—or single? I've looked all evening—and..."

She shrugged, suddenly feeling foolish, because she was asking the hotel help to get her out of the hotel—which wasn't a very good policy.

Much to her surprise the man nodded. "There's an agency just down the street. They open early in the morning. You might try them. They should be able to locate something

115

for you."

She thanked the man and went to her room. Once there, she went to the phone, got the telephone book and started to look up Joe Dickenson's number in the hopes it might be listed. She felt lonely, tired and strangely desperate.

It took only a few moments to find that Joe didn't have a listed number. Tiredly, Ann fell back on to the bed, lonely and frightened for the first time in her life.

Tomorrow she would call Joe, at work, tell him she had moved and how to get in touch with her.

*   *   *   *   *   *   *

Beth Dickenson was dressed in a tight-fitting black cocktail gown, fit to kill. And that was exactly what she planned on doing: killing Joe's resistance to her. It was her only chance. She sat in the car, parked outside of Joe's apartment, waiting for him to come home from work. That way she would really be sure of trapping him. He had never been able to resist her body, never been able to turn her away when she presented her desire to seduce him. Men were easily seduced by a smart woman; they were basically so child-like—put a sex-toy in their face and they couldn't resist. Offer a nice, healthy view of a bulging neckline and their eyes feasted. There wasn't a man alive who could keep from looking at a woman's breasts. She could never fully understand why they found breasts so inviting, so impossible to resist.

She almost laughed at that. Then realized that it was nervousness and the effects of the drinks.

Beth had consumed several Martinis an hour before and the effects were still strong in her system, otherwise it would have been impossible to go through with her plan of desperation. In a short time it would be too late to claim Joe as the father of the life she carried around inside her.

God damn, that bloody ass who did this to me!

She was just taking out another cigarette when she spotted Joe's car coming down the street.

Instinctively she ducked down, so that he wouldn't see her. He might notice the car, but there were plenty of cars like hers.

116

Her ears listened carefully as she waited out the seemingly endless seconds before Joe's car pulled up to the curb outside of the large three-story apartment house where he lived. A door opened and then slammed shut.

Still Beth waited and waited, almost holding her breath for fear she might be discovered too soon.

She was determined to give him time to get into the apartment. Then she'd move to her attack.

Beth waited, while nervously lighting another cigarette. In a way she felt like a real bitch, yet what else was there for her to do? They had enjoyed some nice years together. It wasn't that she didn't love the man. In fact, she half-blamed herself for the failure of the marriage. Turning off sexually to a husband wasn't the best way to make a relationship healthy. Especially when the man had plenty of busty young chicks showing their oversized, surgically enlarged boobs to tempt him into seductive bedroom games. Real stupid on her part.

How could she compete with such competition?

Suddenly she wanted another drink. Her throat was dry, her heart pounding.

Maybe what they had been together, what they had shared, would have some meaning, importance, that could be used to overcome the temptations of his perverse casting coucher's career.

They had enjoyed some wonderful times together. That had to mean something.

Now, if she could convince him she was a changed woman—and once she seduced him and later revealed her condition, maybe things would have a chance of changing. Most men wanted to be a father—and what they didn't know wouldn't hurt them. If Joe thought the child was his, he'd certainly remarry her. Then things would be okay.

Nervously putting out the cigarette, she got out of the car and went across the street to the apartment house. After hesitating a few moments before starting toward Joe's apartment, Beth told herself that what she was about to do was no more terrible than what she had already done with her life and to those around her. They had always wanted a baby, and Joe would never know that it wasn't his. She wouldn't tell him and she'd do everything possible to make certain he never found out the truth.

And she wouldn't be alone any more.

Life was too difficult. And the single world was a terrible place to survive. Once a good marriage had been experienced nothing could possibly replace it. The so-called freedom of the single life was sharply crippled when waking up in bed all alone. And facing the world without a partner to lean upon. She needed a man. She needed Joe.

She stood before the door to his apartment, took a deep breath and then rang the door-bell.

Waited.

It seemed forever before footsteps sounded, then the door opened.

Joe stood there, his mouth open with surprise his shirt half unbuttoned.

"I *had* to see you," she announced simply, forcing her way past Joe, letting a hip brush against him.

There was a long, painful silence while she went into the living room.

Finally the door closed quietly.

Then Joe sighed.

"It's a nice place you have," she observed, casually, controlling the slur of her voice.

"Yeah," Joe admitted awkwardly.

It was the first time she had been to his apartment, and everything seemed strange—almost too strange. But no matter how strange it might be, she had to do what was necessary—or else. She didn't want to think about the "or else" or anything. That terrified her.

The place was furnished in modern pieces and there was a large landscape picture hanging on the wall opposite the entrance.

"What can I do for you, Beth?" Joe inquired in a stiff, awkward voice.

He sounded embarrassed and anxious about something.

"A drink, please?" she asked, turning and looking at him.

He started to say something and then shrugged. "I

don't have much time, Beth. An important...business matter."

He moved to the bar that was used as a divider between living and dining rooms.

Beth nervously considered what she could do. She thought about the men who had given her real parties in the past years. The Las Vegas Beth who was willing to do anything for kicks. That was the Beth that Joe didn't know.

Should she show him that side of her?

No, she told herself. Not that side—not yet, in any case. Unless it was necessary.

Joe handed her a drink and then fixed one for himself.

It was a weak drink, and she stared at it in disgust. Then after a moment gulped it down.

"Please, another."

She extended the glass towards him.

Joe looked up from pouring his own drink, amazement widened his eyes.

"Are you kidding?"

"No!" was her only comment. It was a harsh sound, even in her own ears.

Joe flinched as if slapped mentally. Then he moved the whiskey bottle over her glass, said: "Say when."

She waited until the glass was nearly filled with whiskey before telling him "when" and then reached for it.

Joe frowned as he looked at her from across the bar. His eyes moved to her neckline that revealed enough flesh to be good and sexy. What her breasts lacked in size they made up in firmness and shape. Beth had always been proud of her figure and rightfully so. For a slender woman she had all a man might desire. She was aware of that fact.

As Beth put the glass to her lips and sipped more whiskey, a giggle threatened to burst from her. The thought of being brazenly bold, like she was at Vegas parties, pleased her. Joe would lose his eyeballs with surprise. To him she was still the wife who wouldn't put out. If he only knew about the changes that had taken place, he would really be surprised. But that was something that had to be handled with care. If she were too obvious it would look forced, not

119

natural. Even in her emotional state right now, Beth realized that controlled seduction was mandatory.

"Joe, I've been thinking a lot about us," she finally said. "I don't like the way things are. I tried to get you to understand that the other day, but...maybe I didn't make my point clear enough."

"Beth, what happened in the past—it's part of the *past*. Done with. Finished."

He stared at her for a moment and then looked down at his drink. "What was it you wanted to see me about?"

Beth hesitated, then thought that if she didn't make a move—and fast!—things might never get anywhere.

The liquor was beginning to burn through her brain now, and boldness began to suggest itself. More motivated by desperation than anything else.

Something startling, shocking, that would make its point, was needed. All she had to do was have him seduce her—that was all that was necessary. Then she would claim that he had made her pregnant. As simple as that!

"What was it you wanted to see me about?" Joe repeated again, a little more forceful, more anxious, as if he wished she would get finished with her matter of business.

Beth gulped some more whiskey as her mind formed a daring plan.

Joe had always found her body exciting when it was naked. He had always said that when he saw her figure in the flesh it did things to him that he couldn't control. And how many times when they were married had that been true?

Many, many times. *Any* time he had seen her naked he had been overpowered with wanting to have her.

That had been so annoying that Beth had made a habit to avoid being naked in front of him any more than necessary. She would change in the bathroom, or when he wasn't in the room. Now was the time to take advantage of that power her body had over this man who had been her husband for so many years.

She knew him. Knew the triggers that would fire his body, make him wild with wanting.

There was only one simple action she could take.

"Excuse me, Joe—the girl's room calls!" she laughed

lightly.

Turning, taking the glass of whiskey with her, Beth went across the living room, into the small hall, which was sure to open to bed and bathroom.

* * * * * * *

Joe stood there behind the bar; desperately trying to fight down the irritation that was eating its way through him.

This was all that he needed. Somehow he had to rid himself of Beth—and get the hell out of there. Carol would be screaming if he was late—and that could mean his job and his future. He couldn't take that chance. Yet, what could he tell Beth? It was obvious that his ex-wife was drunk—or damned near it.

He finished off his drink and then started for the bedroom, planning on changing his shirt. That would at least take care of that much time.

As he entered the small square hallway that connected the three rooms, the bathroom door opened and revealed Beth, standing there stark naked.

For a stunned moment he stood there, shocked.

The sight of her body, even more attractive than it had been when they were married, a little more filled out, sent a wave of desire up through him. Memories flooded in his mind of long nights in bed, filled with love, with pleasure, with plans for the future. Home, wife, kids. Everything came back and with them came the desires for home and wife and kids.

It was like being slapped in the face and all he could do was stand there, staring at his ex-wife. Remembering how many years he had wanted her, made love to that body in its younger version. She had been his life, everything he had ever wanted.

Her breasts were still firm and youthful, her figure trim and solid.

"Joe," she breathed huskily, stepping forward, her lithe body moving gracefully, sensually, as she glided to him.

"This is what I wanted—needed!" she murmured,

huskily.

Before he could do anything, her arms were around his neck, her warm breath against his lips, her breasts cushioned tightly to his chest.

It was an erotic contract, and she moved her body in such a way as to accent the erotic. In an amazingly brazen, skilled, knowing manner. Far more confidant than he remembered. There was an intensity of real need revealed in the manner in which she pressed up against him. Her hips locked to his, gently grinding, sensually seducing, not begging, but hungrily seething with real passion, real need, real desire.

This was the woman he had always wanted; the way he'd pleaded with all his heart, prayed for, all those months, even years at the end of their marriage. If only....

"Make love to me, Joe...like you did on our honeymoon. Let me prove to you that things can be like they were in the past, like they were when we had a *happy* marriage. Please let me be a woman again...in your arms, feeling our bodies united in love, in passion, one beautiful union of..."

The words faded as her lips covered his, her tongue attempted to pass his teeth.

The body against his was tensing, her arms tightening around his neck, and it brought back memories of the good days with Beth, and all they had planned together on their honeymoon. The good times.

And suddenly he wanted all those things again, all over again, and the plans and the love and the wife.

He returned her kiss, like a man in a mental fog, his mind whirling dizzily.

How he loved her, his mind chanted. *Oh, Ann, how I love you!*

It was a moment before his confused mind adjusted to that thought. He realized suddenly that the desire to marry, to have a wife, children, home was all centered on another woman. He wanted Ann Farrow, and *not* Beth.

The shock of that realization was so numbing that for a moment he wasn't even aware of the identity of the woman crushing herself against him.

His body was aware of flesh, of a female shape, but

not focused on anything other than the memory of Ann and his continually growing need for her.

How could he love Ann? What had happened to him?

He hardly even knew Ann. Yet, how much did you have to know a woman to love her? He had loved Beth, but in the end everything had gone wrong. He had learned to know her too well, maybe, since then. Too much had happened to him. Nobody stands still; nobody is the same today as they were the day before. To change is to live, and to live is to change. You can't go your life, experiencing life to its fullest, without changes being made. What he and Beth had once had was finished. No matter what might happen right at the moment, or later, the fact was things were totally and completely over between them.

He knew that so clearly now that it was like a pain in his throat.

Suddenly Joe reacted physically to his thoughts, and instinctively, without even realizing what he was doing, he forcefully pushed the woman away from him.

Beth lunged backwards against the wall, and for a moment she stood there, staring at him, her eyes large, and her mouth wide in horror, pain, rejection.

"Joe...Joe..." she finally breathed "What's wrong? Surely you want me. You've always wanted me. You always will. I'm here. Yours. I want you desperately. Need you. You have to love me. Make love to me. Take me...Please. I want you more than anything in the world.... Please! Oh, please!"

Her words broke off. She was breathing hard, then suddenly held her breath as if waiting for his reaction, reply. Her silence pleaded more powerfully than any of the words.

He didn't know what to say. What could he say? It was over. *No, Beth, you are wasting your time. I love somebody else. You are not attractive to me anymore?*

None of that.

Then what?

Nothing. And that's what he said. Nothing at all. And he just stood there, looking at her, in silence, and feeling sick inside because no words could form on his lips. Truth would be more horrid.

He didn't hate Beth any more. He simply didn't care.

She was meaningless. He looked at her body, remembering the good times with a sense of tenderness, but nothing more. He let his eyes caress over her nakedness and all he saw was a lovely woman who was making a fool of herself. He simply didn't want her. He couldn't just take her body in an act of sex without real passion. To abuse her in that manner would pervert the good memories. He did care about her as a human being and as a memory of nicer moments. He cared enough not to want to hurt her any more.

In one way it was like looking at a stranger. A part of him felt nothing other than regret. Pity, maybe, but nothing more than that.

He could see her both ways. As part of a memory— as part of a past dream from which he had awakened. And as a desperate woman who had thrown herself in front of a man and was now facing rejection.

Oh, god, how terrible, he realized. And sad.

"Joe," her voice pleaded, and with that she moved to him again, attempting to put her arms around his neck.

Joe grabbed hold of her wrist, said: "Beth, *don't*, no more!"

"What's wrong?" her voice choked. "Love me ...please, love me. Just do it once. One more time, for memory's sake. So you'll have something wonderful to remember me with."

Strangely he didn't have the desire or caring to even try. Nothing could have caused him to make love to Beth at that moment. She seemed pitiful and suddenly lacking of any sex appeal. And because of that he was puzzled. How could she have meant so much to him in the past, and now nothing?

"Joe, *you have to make love to me! You have to!*" Beth screamed, her face contorting.

"Stop it!" he cried over her yells.

Beth struggled in his grip, and her hips brushed his.

"I know how to do a...lot of dirty things. You'd like me, Joe. You'll like me a lot. I've had men since you—I learned how to please them...you'll think I'm wonderful. Give me a chance...please. Please! Let me suck your dick real hard. Let me make it want to ... *please*, I'll be so

124

good… you'll go crazy. Just like all the other men! I'll make you go wild…you can't believe…what I can make a man do. I'm really great. They all tell me that! I've changed."

Her voice had reached a point of high hysterics. There was an edge of madness in her eyes that was frightening. A desperation that he had never seen there before.

Then suddenly she twisted away from his grip, crushed herself against him, desperately moving her hips in such a way as to excite him. But he felt nothing but disgust.

"Beth!" he yelled, pushing her away again.

Desperately she stared up at him. "I know you'll love it!"

She suddenly dropped to her knees, and her face smothered against his groin.

He grabbed at her, in an effort to stop what she was doing, but instead she moaned in pleasure, believing he was encouraging her. He felt her fingers lowering the zipper and then reaching in and grabbing at him. Before he could stop her, he felt soft, moist lips close greedily on him.

"Yes…yes…" she moaned, "I love…it!"

Disgusted, Joe literally gripped her hair and dragged her away, up, until she was standing once again. "Stop it!"

"Joe. You know you love it. You saw how good I can…be…let me…please." Her hands were now grabbing at him.

He had never known Beth to be that frantic, that aggressive, even that skilled.

But it was too late. He simply didn't care.

This time his right hand slapped across her face in an effort to shock her out of the hysterics.

Her head snapped to one side and then for a moment she stood there staring at him. Then a sob sounded from deep within her, a growing, agonized sob of total defeat and shame. Slowly tears welled in her eyes and then suddenly Beth turned, rushed into the bathroom, slamming the door behind her.

Stunned, he tried to react, tried to feel something other than the confused fury her actions had created in him.

Slowly all feeling ebbed away. Other than the shock at what had just happened.

125

For a long time he waited, hearing in the background Beth's sobs beyond the bathroom door.

And Joe stood there for a long time, now feeling nothing, not even pity.

The sobs from the bathroom annoyed him more than anything else.

He felt sick inside, because life was so damned mixed up now. After this scene all he wanted to do was go out and get drunk and stop thinking. He was mentally numbed, feeling more zombie than man.

What a horrid ending to their relationship.

For a moment, just before turning to enter his bedroom, Joe felt a wave of compassion and emotion toward his ex-wife sobbing in the bathroom but he fought it back, desperately fighting to hold the cold calm of impersonal emotions that had been clouding over him.

Then he turned, went into the living room to the bar, fixed himself a quick shot of whiskey, downed it fast and then went to the bedroom to finish dressing.

The sobbing in the bathroom stopped after a while and then he heard movement of clothing.

He was still numb, feeling nothing, when Beth stepped out of the bathroom. She didn't say anything, but went across the living room. A door opened and then closed.

The closing of the door hit him like an explosion.

The emotion slammed in like the whole room had fallen over his body.

What was happening to his world? His mind screamed desperately attempting to find some logical point to center his emotions and thoughts. Anything other than the pitiful creature that his ex-wife had become.

Then anger took over, a deep, burning anger. He focused on it, fed it, enjoyed it.

The next thing Joe knew was that he had poured himself another drink and was looking into the glass.

Without hesitation he gulped from the glass and then poured himself another strong shot.

He was in the middle of finishing off that drink, when he remembered his command date with Carol Cements.

The anger rushed in again, choking him. His right

126

hand, holding the glass, slammed down on the bar.

Damned women! Goddamned their bloody bodies!

There was nothing to do but go to Carol! But Joe realized there was nothing against going completely smashed.

With that thought he filled the glass again and started getting drunk. He didn't think about Carol. He didn't think about Beth. And most of all he didn't think about Ann Farrow, whom he so desperately loved.

He thought about the job he had to do. Service some bitch in heat. Service CC, the woman any man would desire. Service her body with the necessary thrills on demand. Make love to her as if he meant it.

But it was a job.

Nothing more.

Service a nameless, faceless bitch, and to hell with who it is!

Nothing personal, lady, just part of the job.

He was working. Doing a job. So that he would get ahead in the world.

And that was for himself, and for some special person he didn't want to think about.

CHAPTER THIRTEEN

Carol Clements was slightly drunk, and didn't care. It wasn't the time to be caring much about anything.

She felt a terrible nervousness and anxiety, waiting for Joe Dickenson to turn up. He was already fifteen minutes late.

She was standing next to the bar, a scotch bottle in front of her, the room in semi-darkness, only the bar-light giving a greenish glow to the room. The green color always appealed to her when she was either drunk or sexy. She had never liked red, because it reminded her of her mother.

Mother Whore, tramp-prostitute. Father—unknown!

But Carol Clements had come up in the world. Maybe she put out her body for money, in the beginning—but there was more to it than money. It had been The Career. And she had made it. Any girl in Hollywood had to face up to the fact that prostituting herself was one of the necessities of success. Most didn't call it that. But Carol was wise enough and honest enough within her own mind to believe that's what it really was all about: selling your body for privileges in a still male dominated world. Oh, there were many ways to prostitution. Most women, in fact, just about every woman in the world, had her own personal way and personal rationalization, or name for it. The wife was, as far as Carol felt, nothing but a prostitute—especially when she used sex to have her control over her hubby. *"No goodies tonight, unless you're a nice little boy."* Or maybe she wanted that mink, and so she did her husband up real good, and got the mink. Wasn't that prostitution?

Carol looked into the glass, finding a pleasure in star-ing down into the amber liquid, letting her thoughts run over

129

the many elements and variations of prostitution as she saw it.

Every woman is a whore at heart, her mother had told her over and over again. *I'm just more practical. I'm not tied down with any man, and I got me a nice little girl, too.*

Men made women prostitutes, her mother would continue, *and the smart woman makes the best deal out of it!*

Carol gulped the scotch and cursed bitterly to herself.

And the deal was to keep her body in good shape and use it to control men, to make her way up in the world.

One thing her mother never told Carol was the total joy and pleasures sexual intimacy could give a body. Maybe her mother was frigid; maybe she was highly sexed like Carol. It didn't matter.

Carol had learned, very early, that sex not only worked to get things she wanted, but it also gave her body the special pleasures to match her thrill of controlling men.

So, once she had learned that, she never found it difficult to get a lover to service her on her command, at her beck and call, when she wanted it, how she wanted it and with whom she wanted it. There had been a lot of lovers in her life. And there would be a lot more. They were faceless male animals who serviced her flesh, gave her the thrills she needed. She craved men like the gutter street drunk hungered for booze.

And she didn't lie to herself. She'd used the prostitution game to win in a harsh world. Survival was a bitter struggle against a lot of people who were just as good at the game. You competed with the top of the line in order to get on top. You had to win against all the odds, all the others. And she'd not only played by the rules, but had made a few up along the way.

Prostitution? Well, yes. More like a high priced call-girl who enjoyed her trade.

She gulped men into her life like a thirsty wino sampling all the best wines in the store.

Yeah, and that's sure what I am! A high-class whore. She could call herself that. But nobody else would dare.

So I'm a whore! She laughed in voluptuous amusement. But a high priced, classy, powerful one!

130

Only difference is, I don't get any money from it any more. That is what men call a tramp. A bitch in heat. Whore, pure and simple.

Men, come one, come all, see the glories of CC, the sex-queen of Hollywood, and give her the thrill that the body needs. Free for all—but I'll get a price for the goodies you receive. I make my living using men—and letting them enjoy my body—and letting them give me wonderful, delicious thrills.

But what was the price she was getting from men like Joe Dickenson?

A cheap thrill. But it wasn't so cheap. It was good, *too* good. He was a real man, with real-man hungers. He knew a woman's body, and knew what to do to her.

A needy tremor rushed through her.

"Where the damned hell was he?" she hissed out loud.

Carol looked at her watch. It was half past seven. Half an hour late.

Rotten bastard. What right did he have to stand Carol Clements up? And he better have a good excuse. A damned good one.

Carol dumped the rest of her scotch down her throat, stood and went out onto the patio, looking at the early evening sky.

Life was hell. She had seen it all, from the bottom up.

Carol hated herself, and hated her life. There had been a lot of men in her life, too many to count. And she was tired of the Hollywood scene. Yet, what else was there for her?

Marriage? To whom? Joe Dickenson, or somebody like him? Who would dare to turn her down?

Joe would jump at the chance, she laughed out loud at the thought of his surprised reaction. "Wanna marry me, darling? Come on, let's go to Vegas and sign the papers. I'll make you famous as Mr. Carol Clements!"

Carol laughed, and thought about the idea saying just that to Joe. Really blow his mind! That would be for kicks. Just see if it was possible. It might not be too bad either way. Good for him, fun and kicks for her. Just for a while. A short while to prove that he would do anything she wanted. A voluptuous thrill clutched at Carol.

A love slave, willing to do anything he could to please her; jumping to her every command.

Oh, I love that idea! She thrilled.

That would be wonderful. And good revenge for what men had done to her.

Make him a live-in hubby-slave to her every desire. The dumb jerk was already her slave, helpless. He would lose his job if she snapped her fingers. He would be dropped from the studio if she asked that to happen. And, in fact, she knew that merely not showing up on the set would be enough to ruin his career.

That kind of power almost gave her an orgasm. She shivered. Her hands glided down between her legs, caressing, as she moaned in pleasure. "Oh, dear man...I have you by the balls!"

There was a ringing at the front door.

Carol turned; saw her reflection in the large bay-window that looked into the living room.

She had put on stretch pants and a white blouse. "You have a good figure for a woman in your mid-forties. Even for a woman in her twenties! A damned good one. Sure, not as good as a teenager, but more mature. More knowing about what a man likes to do, and willing to do it." She was in her prime! She laughed and then moved her hands to the top of her blouse, unlatched the top buttons so that it fell free around her breasts.

She had worn a strapless bra that allowed her breasts to appear naked under the opening that the shirt made.

Carol saw Joe step into the living room.

"Out here, darling," she called, waving, attracting his attention.

The man turned, as if groggy, then spotted her. After a moment of staring, he moved toward the double doors that opened into the patio.

"Hello, my dear man, my love-slave," Carol cooed as he stepped up to her. "Oh, that is a turn on! Don't you think?"

The man stood there, less than two yards away, glar-

132

ing at her with red-rimmed eyes, as if angry, as if something inside him were hating her.

"What's wrong? Don't you like what you see?" Carol demanded, harshly.

For a moment it seemed as if he hadn't heard her, then he finally said, swaying slightly as he spoke: "Nothin' shoo shwould under...shand!"

"You're drunk!" Carol laughed, moving in close. "You're drunk!"

She wondered if the man could perform in such condition. He better!

She attempted to put her arms around him and he cursed, almost pushed her away.

"Don't," he yelled, staggering toward the studio door. "I need another drink!"

Anger shot at Carol and then she shrugged. Maybe it didn't have anything to do with her. Maybe it was something personal with him.

Well, it better not get in the way of her joys. She wanted him doing his duty to her body. She needed sex. She was hot and horny.

"Sure, Darling," Carol said, following the man into the studio, playroom.

They sat at the bar, poured drinks and remained silent for some time.

Finally Carol broke the silence.

"Want to talk about it?" she inquired.

"Nothing...to...talk...about." His words came haltingly, pronounced with extreme care.

"Then why aren't you pawing me? I want to be balled, you know that. Now, come on, darling, be a nice guy and service your lady in heat!"

She laughed coarsely at that. A very thrilling sense of power came over her when talking that brazenly to a man over whom she had so much power.

He turned, stared at her. Then his hand reached out and clawed awkwardly at her blouse, ripping it open.

"Is that what you...what?"

"Oh, honey, you don't know how much. Look at me. I'm tingling."

133

Then his fingers found her bra, forced it down, away from her breasts.

He stared at the ends of her breasts and his lips parted. His tongue moistened them.

"Like what you see, darling?" she murmured in pleasure.

"What are you?" he finally asked in a wondering voice.

"What kind of question is that?" Carol snapped, taking a deep breath, which pushed out her naked breasts. She leaned close pressed one breast into her arm.

"They could use a little loving, Joe," she murmured, looking up into his eyes. "I've waited for you."

Suddenly she remembered that she had been forced to wait for over thirty minutes for him.

"You kept me waiting," Carol said in a much too soft a voice. Strangely there was no anger in her right then, only a craving that her body was now warming up to like a hot poker in red-hot coals.

"Tough!" Joe fairly growled. "So...you waited."

"I don't like waiting!"

"Waiting makes a lady hotter!" he announced. His voice was level, his eyes bright, but his attitude was strangely different. The man was, obviously, drunk but also seemed quite in control. Yet even then there was vagueness in his manner. He just stared at her.

"I'm hot enough to fry you to a crisp!" she taunted him, with a laugh. "Burn you alive."

He continued to stare at her, not moving.

"Don't you want me? Are you just going to look? I need it, Joe. You know how bad I need it. So...deliver... come on, big boy. I want you. Tell me how much you want me."

"Yes, yes, sure I want you, too...yes, yes," his voice was chanting like a recording, almost on automatic. "Who wouldn't want the famous CC?"

"Yes...you lucky man. Take advantage of me, if you must!" she fairly laughed in his face, partly inventing the corny dialog, but basing it on some long forgotten script. "I'm a hot momma wantin' me daddy to make me scream in

134

joy. You're a hot dog burning hard and big...oh, holy doggie mine!"

Then she reached hungrily for him, suddenly out of control, unable to stop the overwhelming need that had been building up for far too long. The day at the studio had been straining. And now the reward was in her hands. Her body surged hotly against his, greedy, excited, desperate.

Carol would have said more but he suddenly smothered them down her throat.

The embrace was so fast, his tongue so demanding in its deep kiss, that Carol felt suddenly stunned.

A voluptuous need built up in her, so strong that she wanted to rip the clothing from his body and have him do it to her right there on the bar stool. She was all at once enveloped in sensations, fiery, squeezing around her like some powerful cloud, fingers gripping her body in thrilling pleasure. Every nerve was feeding on the impending delicious release, knowing that it was only moments before he'd be really at her, really in her, a part of her body.

"Love, love me," she moaned when the kiss broke. "Love me hard!"

An animal sound came from his lips, which was mostly a curse of anger. He stood and jerked her from the bar stool. She felt herself being shoved toward the couch. And she was overwhelmed in the pure joy, pleasure, and excitement at being taken by this suddenly crazed wild man. She literally felt voluptuous orgasms shudder though her. Even his words meant nothing other than being thrillingly overwhelming.

"I'll stud you...like a damned whore!"

Carol felt herself fall down against the sofa and then felt a wave of excitement as the man fell almost brutally on her. His hands were sending waves of excitement through her body as they fairly tore the clothing away to expose naked flesh to feast upon.

* * * * * * *

Joe was swimming in a daze, in a sea of drunkenness, hardly aware of where he was, whom he was with.

He remembered vaguely having come to Carol Cements house, and then fairly attacking her in the playroom.
But time and space had become mixed up.

She was in his arms, trembling, frantically clinging,
hungrily devouring, clawing at him, her hands eager to find
new strength in his body, her form, like soft hot silk, mold-
ing itself to his.

Everything was confused in his mind. Time blurred,
then ecstasy swelled up in him and exploded.

He was floating in black water, yet falling, falling
downwards through ink night, stars surrounding him.

A face was suddenly close to him, it was smiling,
lovingly.

"Marry me, Joe...marry me," the voice said, and he
remembered that he wanted to get married. But, no! Not to
Beth. Never to her again.

Marry Ann. Oh, yes, how he wanted to marry Ann
Farrow, more than anything else in the world. He needed her
so much. And how beautiful she seemed, looking down at
him, smiling, begging him to marry her.

He reached for the body that must surely go with the
face, and then slowly pulled the dear form to him.

"Oh, dearest, I've waited," he heard his own voice
scream through the blackness, seemingly to echo back at him
from a hallow cave. "Want...you."

"Love, love...love me for ever and ever. Marry me,
Joe...marry me, and you'll have everything you want. Everything!" the woman's voice pleaded as hands caressed the
back of his neck. "I want you more than anything in the
world."

"Yes," he agreed. "Oh, yes..."

"We'll be together forever. You'll be my loving
slave."

"Yes...forever..." he repeated, totally dazed about
what was happening. But it was all taking place in a deep
well, and he felt so distant from the woman's voice. Frantically he reached tighter around her naked body, thrilling to the
soft, hot flesh, the voluptuous wonderful woman who loved
him so much, who wanted to marry him forever, to be his
wife, and have his children and...

136

"Oh, yes, fuck me hard!" she moaned. "Love me hard!"

That was jarring, exciting, but strange sounding.

Something was wrong, but he couldn't understand what. Maybe it was the drinks. He felt sick inside and at the same time joyous.

She loved him and wanted him, and would marry him.

"With me...it'll be...so...perfect!" She gasped as their bodies surged together. "I promise you, darling. Like this...always. Like...oh, like this... Promise you!"

Something about the voice, the tone, the words felt all wrong, but her body simply took control of his, fairly leaping up, surrounding him, enveloping him, draining furiously on all that was flaming painfully hard through every muscle, nerve, cell. She was literally devouring his total being. He was being sucked into her furnace like some whirlpool had simply wrapped itself about him, twisting, tangling, churning demanding with such force that nothing else existed in the dark depths of his mind.

Then mere animal sensations took over and everything seemed to blur, disappear into a daze of movement that he was not really able to understand.

How long that lasted he didn't know. But the next thing was the reality of slowly, slowly climbing up through darkness, with pain surrounding him, pounding at his brain, at his head as if there were hammers attempting to crush his skull.

* * * * * * *

Beth didn't really know where she was. Some street without a name. Somewhere distant from the scene of Joe's apartment.

The sickness was still there, eating at her like the child that was in her stomach.

What had happened to her life and her future? There wasn't any, really. There couldn't be. The father was gone, the husband, who wasn't a husband any more, was gone. All the past was dead. Finished for her.

Beth knew that the Martinis had made her drunk, yet strangely enough her thoughts seemed clear.

There had been many thoughts running through her mind. Shame thoughts.

Shame at what she had become; shame at what she had done with Joe. More shame because he had turned her down.

What was wrong? He had always desired her body. He had always wanted her. Or had he lied? Had it all been a lie? After all, Joe had been the one to go out and seek other women.

Beth wanted to run and run and never stop running. The world seemed to be choking around her life, as if tangling her in a terrible web from that it was impossible to escape.

Oh, if there was only some such escape. If only she could find a way out. If only she could go back, start over, knowing what she knew now. Why? Why had she done all those things? In Vegas. Making a tramp out of herself. It would have been better to have let Joe have her when they were married.

That had been the first mistake. The second had been sleeping with any man willing to give her a thrill.

She should have been a decent wife to Joe. She had wanted that. But hadn't known how. But there was no excuse. She could have faked it. Could have lied. Could have appeared to be something she never wanted to be. A lie.

If anything, Beth had always tried to be honest with herself.

Like now. It was all her fault. She'd screwed up. Everything was wrong.

But why? What had gone wrong?

Vegas had taught her so much. But too late. She knew, oh so well, how to please a man and how to enjoy it. All she had to do was walk into any bar and there would be somebody to service, to feast upon.

Oh, God what have I become?

Now she couldn't really remember the reasons she had sought out thrills. Cheap thrills given cheaply by nameless fathers.

Beth felt the urge for another drink, and another dip into the escape from reality that was now choking her mind with pain and anguish.

She wanted to simply die. End it all. Wash all the pain away. It was impossible to have the child. Abortion wouldn't resolve things, either. Some women could do that. She simply couldn't. And she couldn't have the baby.

What was left? What could a woman in her position do?

She had failed at everything. And there was only one escape from that failure.

It wasn't going to be easy to kill herself. And Beth had the terrible feeling that it would be impossible.

But that was the only solution to her problem. It was quite simple.

No baby without a father. No abortion. Then death was the only escape. And burning in hell.

Her Catholic-raised mind rebelled from all that. And at the same time embraced the horrible reality that was going to be hers.

She had to act. And now. Tonight. Not another day needed to go by. She couldn't face the pain and humiliation.

Her eyes focused on the street. She searched for a bar. There were a lot of them around. But the one across the street, the one with the red lettering saying "Joe's Place" fairly drew her across the street. What a wonderful place to start the final event in her life.

Beth stepped off the curb, walked toward the bar with the title of "Joe's Place."

All her thoughts were centered on finding *Joe's Place,* because it was much easier that way. Far more easy.

Find Joe's place and then escape in his arms, in his love, like it had been years before, when they had been happy and in love, with the future looking beautiful and perfect.

If only it had worked out like that, Beth thought bitterly. *If only...*But there were too many "if only's" in her life and it was impossible to go back and change them. Too many roads that led to forks and wrong turnings.

Beth didn't hear the sound of traffic and didn't hear

the screech of brakes. Too much of her attention was centered on finding Joe's place, that one place where she had been happy, young and with the future to look forward to.

Her thoughts were frozen to the memory of what it had been like—and the dream of what it might have been like, if certain things hadn't happened.

And that's when the car hit her, lifting her body upwards, high over it. Vaguely Beth was aware that something was wrong. It was suddenly too cold, too dark. Sensation was gone, numbed in one explosion of sensation that she wasn't able to understand.

Maybe she was going back in time, back to when they were happy together, when everything had a future to look forward to.

Then suddenly her body hit the street, some ten yards from where the car had struck her. In that instant a thought died, ended instantly, without pain, without awareness of what had really happened.

Just...

The End.

CHAPTER FOURTEEN

Joe felt like some kind of zombie. His head was fighting the battle of the bulge; his mouth was dry paste, like some kind of coated desert, as he walked into his office at the *Bennick Studios.*

He had left Carol Clements at the Makeup Department. The major thing, Joe kept telling himself, was Carol was at work on time. His stud job of the night before had been, apparently, clean and had worked. He didn't remember much.

He walked past June without saying a word. He was just sitting in a chair when June came up, handed him a cup of coffee.

He looked up into her eyes and tried to thank her silently.

June was a good secretary; knew where and when not to talk. Knew his needs without having been told.

Joe sat there, looking at the steaming coffee, trying to remember the night before. Everything was distant and puzzling, like he had been sleep-walking.

After the scene with Beth, Joe had gone out and gotten himself drunk at a bar near Carol Clements' home. One more drink in the bar and he wouldn't have made it to her place.

After arriving, having the drink with Carol, he remembered little. They had had sex. How he had managed, Joe didn't know. Liquor could kill a man's sex-machine. But his had strangely continued; functioned without any effort from his conscious mind.

Then the dream. Memory of that made him sit up straight. The action hurt his head, sending hammers through

141

his skull.

His lips moaned automatically, but his thoughts were clear, sharp.

He was in love with Ann Farrow.

Of course, that was fantastic. Even admitting it to himself seemed fantastic.

All morning long his thoughts were centered on Ann Farrow. Several times he asked June if she had received any communication from Ann, but the answer was negative.

It wasn't until about 11:40 that morning that June told him there was a call from a Miss Farrow.

Like a man possessed, Joe jumped, as if shot.

"Hello," he said after picking up the receiver. The voice was music to his ears.

"Hi, I just called to tell you I've moved...found a place on Lexington, not far from Hollywood and..." Her voice trailed off, then picked up, nervously. "I guess you think I'm terribly bold and all that, but I—"

"Stop right there, Ann." Joe controlled the emotion in his voice, telling himself it was silly to feel so excited. "Where are you now? Are you doing anything for lunch?"

"No."

"Then I'll see you in half an hour," he fairly shouted into the receiver.

She told him where to pick her up and then they said good-bye.

Joe went out to June, said: "I'll be out late...if there isn't anything on the boards."

June looked through his appointment pad. "Lunch with a Miss Thornton."

Joe shook his head. "Call her, say I can't make it. Anything else?"

The woman shrugged.

"Nothing on the books. Where will I be able to get you?" she inquired knowingly.

"I don't know."

"What about Carol?"

He was silent for a moment, then shrugged. "I guess she can't be mad if I'm on business."

June looked doubtful.

142

"To hell with her!" he snapped angrily, turning, starting back into his office. Then he reconsidered.

"I'll see you later," he announced, starting for the exit. "Hold off any appointments, any women—I think you can handle that, can't you?"

"Carol?"

"Well...tell her I'll call later—don't say where I'll be...don't commit me to a time or place. She can sweat it out."

"You sure?"

"Well, okay, say..." desperately he struggled, then sighing, defeated, he shrugged.

She suggested: "I'll tell her you can't wait to see her. That you're pantin' and hungry to be in her arms."

He gaped at her.

"Oh, come on, Joe, it isn't a secret. And I'm on the inside track. You're being forced to stud for her."

"Shit."

"Well, you're protecting both of our jobs, aren't you?"

"Christ!"

"Can it be all that bad?"

"Are you kidding?"

"The famous CC just panting and ranting and hungry for your big wonderful bod? That has to be some trip!"

"Oh, now she tells me."

"What?"

"That you think I'm hot."

"Did I say that?" she beamed with humor.

"You said I have a wonderful big bod."

"No. Big wonderful bod!"

"What's the dif?"

"Just quote me correctly. And you *are* a wonderfully build male animal." Her eyes ogled his body as if wanting to devour it. She was all satire and grinning hard at him.

"And how come you never wanted to make use of it?"

"I wanted to keep you as a fantasy. No man can live up to a woman's fantasy. Not even you."

"I wish CC felt the same way."

"She's not very picky-picky, so I've been told."

"Oh, thanks. Thanks a load. Compliments deluxe!"

"Well, that's a load off my body, darling!"

"Oh, God, now you sound just like CC."

"I tried, honestly I did." She grew suddenly serious at that point: "I'll tell your hot little bitch what she wants to hear most coming from your very lips. Will that help?"

"Just so you don't get me married to the woman."

"Heaven forbid. I'd marry you myself, first, before letting her get her claws into you like that," she announced.

"Promises, promises. All big mouth as usual!" he managed with humor. The exchange had lightened things slightly. That—mixed with the fact that he'd have Ann in his arms in a very few minutes. He was actually happy, thrilled, light hearted, alive!

"I'm all mouth, so they say!" she murmured with a slight smirk. "But a good one, so I've been told."

"You make that sound..."

"Keep it clean! I'm a good girl. I don't go for those...nasty little naughty things people do to one another...I'll put soap in your mouth, if you don't watch out!"

"You're the best, really."

"I know. That's why you're studding for CC—just to keep me happy on the job!"

He chuckled, winked at her and said: "Well, shame you aren't willing to—"

"Now keep it clean. Soapy, soapy. I have a bar right here."

"And I bet it would be delicious coming from you!" he laughed.

"You know I'm a pure, innocent lady, a maiden who does not play office games with her boss! Arms' distance and all that."

"Damn shame that!" With that parting shot, Joe opened the door and went into the hallway, determined to make himself hard to find for the next half hour.

That was the one advantage of his job; he could disappear for an afternoon, and say it was some kind of business and, if necessary, get an agent to back up his story. Agents liked to please people in his type of position. It was good for business.

He was humming as he got into his car a few moments later.

* * * * * * *

Ann felt strangely excited after hanging up the phone. She turned and looked at the furnished apartment to make sure everything looked good.

"Of course it does," she told herself.

It was a modern apartment and in the bedroom were her suitcases, still packed. The first thing she had done was to call Joe's office. She hadn't expected that he would move so fast. Now there was so much to do and not enough time.

They would have to have drinks before they went out to lunch. Here, in the apartment.

Her head was swimming. One half hour just wouldn't be enough time.

Ann quickly left the apartment and went down the corner to a liquor store. There she bought a bottle of expensive Scotch and two glasses, and a bottle of soda water. Joe liked Scotch, and she planned on pleasing him to the best of her ability.

There was a glowing flush to her cheeks as she reentered the one bedroom apartment she had rented that morning.

Ann put the bottles and glasses in the small kitchen and then rushed to the bedroom, opened one of the three suitcases, and started pulling out clothing as fast as possible, looking for her green dress that opened at the back, and had a revealing neckline.

This meeting with Joe had to have impact, hit him where it would do the most good. He was her only contact, now.

As Ann got undressed, there was the sound of footsteps outside and then a knock.

Frantically she looked at her wristwatch.

He was early. Oh, why did he have to be early?

"Just a second!" Ann called, hurriedly searching for a morning robe. It took several minutes to find the robe in the

145

second suitcase. This she quickly threw around her, forgetting to pull the belt tight.

As she rushed to the door the robe fell loose around her body. She stopped, started to tie the robe shut and then decided against it.

Joe had seen her completely naked before. She was almost respectably dress, with bra and panties.

Ann opened the door, keeping herself behind it so that nobody from the outside could see her.

Joe stepped in, a grin on his features.

"Hi, where are you?" he greeted.

Ann slammed the door shut and he turned, stared.

A flush rushed up Ann's cheeks as she saw his eyes sweep her body.

"You caught me unprepared," she explained.

His eyes twinkled, as if saying, "I just bet!

"No, honestly," she cried, almost pleading for him to believe her.

"I didn't say a thing," he said.

"I could read your thoughts!" Ann felt another flush surge across her face.

"Why are you getting so embarrassed?" he accused, grinning.

"I'm *not* embarrassed," Ann announced, knowing her voice was harsh, high pitched and *very* embarrassed sounding.

His eyes looked at her bra, where her breasts pressed together. "You are even more beautiful than I remembered!"

"You either are giving me a line, or have a very short memory," she laughed, recovering some of her composure again.

"Neither. Just that you grow more beautiful every time I see you," Joe told her, stepping closer.

Ann backed against the wall and felt very helpless and small. It was a delightful feeling, one that she hadn't experienced for some time.

"You sure know how to hand a girl a line and..."

Joe was too close, his lips already only inches from hers and she broke off, hypnotized, a sudden wanting starting to develop in her.

146

Then just as he was about to kiss her, Ann laughed, coyly pushed him away. "Now, none of that!"

Joe quickly moved back, turned, said: "I'm sorry."

"I have to change. How about fixing us some drinks in the kitchen. There...there's a bottle and glasses.

"That and soda water." She moved toward the bedroom, said: "I'll be back, soon."

* * * * * * *

Joe fought back the almost overwhelming urge to follow Ann into the bedroom. His every nerve cried out to make love to her right then and there. He wanted to hold her, touch her, kiss her, simply smother her with caresses.

He hadn't been handing her a line. The words had flooded out, and there were so many others that he wanted to say. Only sanity caused him to hesitate. No woman could believe him if he said he loved her after only having seen her just a few times. It was just too hard to believe, even for himself.

Joe went into the small kitchen, found the bottle of Scotch and opened it. But his thoughts were in the bedroom with Ann. He couldn't get the idea out of his mind, the craving and demanding idea to go in there and embrace that wonderful body. To literally envelop her into his arms.

He was holding two glasses of scotch, walking across the living room, toward the bedroom, when he suddenly realized what he had already planned on doing.

Without breaking pace, Joe continued up to the door, which was closed.

He stood there, both glasses in his hands and not knowing how to open the door.

For a long time he stood there, listening to the movements in the other room, wanting to be in there with Ann.

A hard lump choked his throat as he pictured that wonderful body held next to his, naked, warm, giving, wonderful.

It was so strange, so impossible, and yet too damned good. Joe was old enough and experienced enough to know

147

the signs. They were for real. He was simply and totally mad about her.

Then he did a stranger thing.

Turning, Joe went to the low, green sofa, sat down, put the two drinks on the coffee table in front of him and sat there waiting.

He had finished his second cigarette when the bedroom door opened.

Looking up, Joe gasped.

Ann stood there in a dark green dress that hugged her figure in such a way as to show off every curve, every swell.

That lump hardened in his throat.

Her breasts were high, pushing out against the dipping neckline. It was more an evening dress than an afternoon luncheon dress, but he didn't care. In fact he couldn't have been more delighted. It would be possible to sit there staring at her all afternoon.

Words flooded to his lips, but no sound came out. What could he say? That she was beautiful? That would hardly have been enough. It wouldn't have been even a beginning.

Her lips, red silk, moist, shining, kissable, half parted. Her eyes were green, haunting, eager, and bright. Her blonde hair like gold around her face, framing it in such a way as to accent her features in a most attractive way.

"I'm sorry it took so long," she said, gliding toward him. The movement was both sensual and natural.

It had rhythm and beauty that hypnotized him.

It's funny, Joe thought, as she settled down beside him, reaching for the drink he had fixed for her, *how much a man can miss when first seeing a woman.*

It seemed that every time he looked at Ann there was some new feature, some new effect and some new magic to reach out and cast its spell over him. She was like a drug that ripped through his own being.

How he wanted to tell her what he was feeling right then. But that was impossible. No words would express it fully.

So fast, his mind admitted dizzily.

"How do you like me?" she inquired in a teasing

voice, her eyes flashing as they met his in a warm, intimate gaze.

"You've never looked more beautiful." Joe reached for his glass, gulping almost nervously.

"Come on, now, you almost sound like you mean it," Ann countered.

"I do."

"I hope so," she told him, grinning happily. She leaned closer, touching his lips with delicate, red painted fingernails. "I really hope you like me."

Emotion touched his voice when he said: "I like you a lot, Ann."

That's nice, her eyes silently said.

"More than nice, Ann...much more," he whispered half to himself. "God you're lovely!"

They sat there for some time in silence, finishing their drinks. She asked for a cigarette and he lighted one for her, after which he placed it gently between her lips.

There was something wonderfully intimate and sensual about that action that sent a wave of excitement through Joe. How he wanted to crush her to him. But suddenly he felt like a little schoolboy on his first date. He had a terrible feeling of awkwardness, which made it almost impossible to do or say anything.

That was a sure sign that something was happening—something very important.

He looked into her green eyes and tried to see if she felt the same thing. But there was only an innocent expression there, revealing nothing.

Joe tried to tell himself that this was all foolish. After all, Ann was a woman he had met at a party and then shacked up with for the weekend. They had been in bed since then. Why should he suddenly feel such awkwardness? He wanted to make love to her, right there, now, without waiting through a lunch. He wanted to take her in his arms, and feel her dear body pressed against his and know the warmth of her, the thrilling ecstasy of their forms locked in a love embrace.

There was nothing holding him back.

Joe started to lean toward her, planning on taking her

in his arms. But instead he stood, without even thinking, and said: "Let's get the hell out of here and have something to eat."

Ann looked startled, then smiled. "Why, Joe, that's a wonderful idea." She stood, moved toward the door. "For a moment there I could have sworn you were about to rape me!"

Joe tried to sound light, casual as he countered with: "Now, how in the world could you have gotten that idea?"

"I'll never tell," she laughed, opening the door and waiting for him.

He came up to her, then started outside, hesitated, retreated, kicked the door shut and then pulled Ann into his arms.

She came easily against him, looking up into his eyes, her lips parted, her eyes half lidded, waiting.

His lips touched her and it seemed as if some magic worked over him.

It was completely different than any kiss he had experienced before with Ann. It wasn't sexual, while being the most sexual kiss in the world. It was emotion and love and affection and everything combined into one bang.

Her body strained against his, but not too boldly.

More like a woman giving herself fully to him, not in a greedy, savage way, but in a loving totality.

After a long moment the kiss ended and they clutched to each other, as if clinging to life itself. Their breaths were coming heavily and he felt suddenly weak and exhausted. Trembling.

Slowly, very slowly, they moved away from each other and their eyes locked in an intimate gaze. He was sure he read emotion in her eyes, deep, hungry and tender emotion. But he wasn't completely sure.

Without a word he opened the door and the two of them stepped outside, as if controlled by one mind.

There was a time for love and there was a time for other things. Strangely this wasn't the time for love. It was the time to be two people, learning about one another, being with one another and doing things together. Experiencing the true meaning of love.

150

Passion would come later, as it should, when the time was ripe. Right now just being together, close, as a couple. Not two people on the make.

As they started toward his car Joe knew, without any reservations, that he was very much in love with Ann Farrow. And he didn't give a damned about her past, about how they had met, or anything other than this was the woman he wanted to be with the rest of his life. The woman he wanted to marry.

Parley in Passion, by Charles Nuetzel

CHAPTER FIFTEEN

Ann felt simply wonderful and kept trying to tell herself that this was all some kind of make-believe and that it wasn't as important or exciting as it might seem.

They were sitting in a darken restaurant, sipping after lunch cocktails. And it had been one of the most pleasant lunches she had ever experienced.

It was all too glowing. So perfect.

"What ever happened between you and Mari?" Joe inquired, tapping an ash into the ashtray between them on the table.

"Oh, just a falling out, that's all," she quickly said, hoping that would satisfy him.

Joe gave her a prolonged look, as if attempting to read her mind.

"What really made you come to Hollywood, Ann?"

"The movies. Always wanted to get into the movies." She looked away nervously suddenly feeling ill-at-ease, partly because movies and acting seemed so far away, so distant and out of focus.

"Ann, have you ever thought what it might cost you as a person...going into acting?" Joe inquired carefully.

"I guess, a little. Some hard work and—"

"Had any acting experience?"

"Not to speak of but—"

"Going to school—acting, taking lessons?"

"No...hadn't got around to that. I was told that with the right backing, with the right contact, a girl could get ahead in the business. That all it took was promotion," Ann admitted, feeling foolish. "I haven't had a chance to work all the details out. Not that I'm foolish or stupid. Just that, well,

153

things have been happening terribly fast."

Joe slowly shook his head from side to side. "Ann, it can be done like that. Mari did it that way...but where is Mari? Just a bit actress and that's all she ever will be. Men like that kind of woman around and they will keep her around by handing out the bait. It sounds cruel, but the world is cruel and—"

"Well, I only got here a few weeks ago, really and haven't had a chance to look into what was necessary to do and—"

"Ann, it takes a lot of work. Sweat. And your life is not your own. Carol Clements is a perfect example of what can happen to a girl. Carol worked hard and slept her way up—and made it. That doesn't mean all women have to take that track. Just that many do. And there are so many that are talented, well prepared and still struggling as waitresses. The numbers are staggering. And talent is cheap. To be frank. And beautiful women are all over the place. They come here like sheep, flocks of them almost daily, seeking to make their break into show-biz. And they get nowhere. It can be a dead end street to horrible frustration and terrible disappointment. Very few get past the studio front gate. Far less into bit parts. The numbers are staggering. Even the big names struggle. And you can't keep on the top without paying a terrible place. People like Carol Clements are a perfect example of the difficulties of trying to keep a career going. Women have it harder, cause after a very young age they are already too old. Men can get away with wrinkles. Women can't. And...well even then there are other hellish issues. With Carol...well she's slipping, and she has never been really happy. She'll end up nowhere, slowly shuddering into the sunset of her life, alone and still hungry and desperate for the power she once had. Maybe she'll get married several times—but no man will be able to please her long. And Carol Clements isn't the exception.

"It is hard to make a go at it in Hollywood. If a career is really what a woman wants—fine. But what do you really want, Ann? Have you actually ever given it any deep thought?"

Ann sat there, not knowing if she should be mad or

154

pleased. Joe was giving her some basic facts. He seemed to care. His eyes, his voice, what he said seemed to indicate great caring.

"I don't know, Joe...just that—well, things seemed to drift in this direction. I made contacts, learned about Mari and that she was willing to help others and..."

"Forget Mari."

"Well, if it weren't for her I'd never have met you."

"That's true, but...where will that get you?" he asked pointedly.

She stared at him, confused, not certain what he meant. She felt a sense of guilt about Mari, even while being furious at the woman. It didn't seem fair to be talking about her so negatively behind her back.

"I don't know, to be honest," she stated, evasively. "I'm just glad we met."

"Oh, yes! So am I! You have no idea!" he quickly said, taking her hand, holding it in his on the table between them.

"Yes...but what can I do for you?" he quickly continued, before she could answer his question. "I can help you, in time. But I'm struggling to get into production. I could get you the right press agent, and start you in the right direction in-so-far as getting acting, dancing instructions, etc. And you *are* just about the most beautiful woman I have ever known."

"Oh, come on, now."

"No, I mean that."

"Surely you have—"

"This isn't the time to be handing out a line. I'm just trying to find out where you stand, and what you *really* want out of life. If you want acting more than anything else, more than personal happiness in marriage and children, that's fine. That's a choice. And there's nothing saying that you can't have both. But not necessarily in that order. To become an actress, making money—a living, there is a lot that you have to do. And your life won't be your own. Believe me in that. You will have to eat, sleep and live acting 48 hours a day, 14 days a week—if you know what I mean." He lighted a cigarette and then continued: "You can't have your cake and...well, eat it, too. You have to give up one hell of a lot—

and I sometimes think women are crazy to give up so much. You have to understand the risks, the challenges, the price tag that is demanded. And the chances of success are balanced against the better chance of failure. It just isn't worth it. For a man—that's something else. He has to make a living for the rest of his life. Regardless of fem issues, and all that … the fact still remains that for most vast populations world wide all a woman has to do is find a husband and—"

"Raise children," Ann announced heatedly. "What's wrong with a woman having a career? What's wrong with a woman having dreams of being somebody and doing things creatively? What says a woman just has to be a housewife and mother? I don't think that is all that I want. I want more. I want a man who can support me and love me—and I want children—but I want to be somebody, too. That's what is important to me. Stand on my own feet, not dependent, pregnant and fat!" she blurted those words out with real furious emotion.

"And that's why I came to Hollywood in the first place. To find a place of importance for myself!" She fairly spat out the words, and was breathless when finished.

They sat there staring at each other for a long time, as if strangers. Then Joe sighed, said: "That still doesn't answer my question. What do you really want out of life? That is the important thing."

He was thoughtful for a moment. Then shrugged "I'm sorry, I guess I'm asking myself the same question. A lot has happened to me, personally, in the last days and...I guess I have to ask that question over and over again until some answer comes!"

Suddenly Joe looked at the check that the waitress had placed on the table, then said, "Let's get out of here!"

As they were getting into his car, Ann asked: "What are *you* looking for in life, Joe?"

He started the car and then headed into traffic, moving in the direction of her new apartment, before saying anything.

"I don't know for sure. I have to make a living. But I want something more than what I've had and something more than life seems to have for me in the offering, as of

156

now!" His voice was thoughtful, and slightly violent.

"What would that be?" she wondered out loud.

Joe turned and looked at her for a moment, their eyes meeting for a split second, but there was something in his which sent a tingling sensation through Ann.

"I guess I want what most men want."

"And that would be?" Ann pushed, wondering why it was so important to find out.

"I guess..." His voice faltered for a long moment and they had driven three blocks before he continued. "A wife...kids, I suppose."

The silence was heavy after that until they came to a stop in front of her apartment.

They sat there for some time before saying anything.

Ann broke the silence.

"You'll come up for a drink?" she offered, feeling that her voice was a little too shaky.

"Yes, I'd like that," Joe told her in a very, very quiet voice.

As they entered her apartment, she told Joe to fix the drinks while she changed.

"The dress is a little tight," she laughed.

"I guess it is—beautifully tight," Joe countered, smiling.

She went into the bedroom, closed the door, and leaned back against it, her breath suddenly short, and her thoughts steaming violently.

What did she really want out of life? What was really important?

Happiness, she guessed. *But what was happiness?*

Ann shook her head, dazed by the maze of thoughts that were teeming through her mind, unable to think rationally.

She sighed, stepped toward the bed and started to change. She would have to move the suitcases, for surely they would soon be in each other's arms making passionate love on the bed. She wanted that so badly that the very thought caused an uncontrolled tremor to rush through her.

That would be so good because of so many, many reasons.

Mainly because Joe was a wonderful lover and wonderful man.

Because she wanted him to make love to her.

But also because the confusion of her thoughts would be blurred away with passion.

Enveloped within his strong, powerful arms holding her close, his body possessing her totally.

Oh. Now that's for sure, what she wanted more than anything else that she could imagine.

Just get lost in this wonderful man's arms and forget everything else. That's all that mattered.

* * * * * * *

For Joe everything was moving so fast that he felt mentally numb. He wanted desperately to ask Ann to marry him, but was sure that she would turn him down, flat. They hardly knew each other. And a marriage right then might be complicated.

In the kitchen he poured the drinks and downed one of them, refilling the glass.

It seemed to take forever before Ann returned from the bedroom. By that time he was in the living room sitting on the sofa, his eyes closed and his thoughts still playing with the idea of being married to Ann, wondering what it would be like. He couldn't get the desire out of his mind. It was almost an insane drive to have it out with Ann, once and for all, to know one way or another if there was any chance and if they could, in time, at least, become man and wife.

How desperately he needed to know that.

When she opened the bedroom door, Joe didn't move, didn't open his eyes.

Instead, he waited for her to come to him, to see what she would do.

They were to make love, that was simple enough and the very maturity of this fact was pleasantly exciting. No words, no statement. It was as simple as breathing.

He heard the footsteps and then felt the pressure of her form move down next to him on the sofa.

Then suddenly her lips touched his cheek.

"Hello," she greeted brightly. Joe opened his eyes and looked at her.

The sight was stunning. He knew they would make love, but wasn't quite sure how Ann would go about it.

Instead of changing into something casual, instead of putting on a filmy nightgown, she had done the most direct and bold act possible.

Her beautiful nude figure rested close to his and suddenly the desire to hold her tight, to cover her lips, to escape his thoughts in the passion her body could offer and give, was an overwhelming power over him.

Strange, he thought, how people were, how they would act under the right conditions. Before, she had been shy, even embarrassed when he had come to the apartment and she was wearing an open robe and bra and panties. But now the situation was different. She had come to him as a mature woman, willing to give fully of herself, naked, ready for his lover's embrace.

Joe moved without even knowing he was moving. All of a sudden she was in his arms, cradled gently, her warm body soft and yielding against his.

She opened her mouth to his and tensed as his tongue probed deep, hungrily, but so tenderly.

How he loved her. How impossible it was *not* to love her. There didn't have to be any logic. There simply had to be a desire to need, a desire to be needed, a desire to love and there it would be, right to the point, without logic being necessary—or reason.

Why should he ever stop to reason or think? Tell or express what he felt. Let her know that he loved her more than any woman in the world; that he wanted her to be his wife, and live with him for the rest of their lives.

But the words didn't come, because right then they were out of place. Words needed not to be shared. Just emotion, feeling, sounds, but soft, murmuring sounds of love, of two lovers embracing, becoming aware of all they were together.

Without speaking, Joe slowly stood, pulling her up with him. Then he lifted her into his arms, burying his lips into the soft cream of her throat, gently kissing as he moved

159

toward the bedroom.

How he was going to love her. Love her like he had never made love to a woman. With tenderness, with care, with gentle caresses and kisses until she raged in his arms, until her form was hot fire fairly screaming to be released from the burn of passion.

Then he would move to her and fully possess that lovely body, blending them both into one body and soul in the final act of love and ecstasy

As he came to rest in front of the bed, Joe slowly leaned down and placed Ann gently on the bed.

For a long time he stood there looking at her, marveling over her lush, beautiful, firm body, a body that he loved more than any other; one he wanted to possess forever. A woman he wanted to possess him in total.

Her eyes looked up at his and there was deep welling emotion there, as if reaching out to caress him, as if reaching for his soul and attempting to say all those intimate things that true lovers the world over have always said in moments of truth.

Slowly, carefully, he undressed and then finally slipped down onto the bed next to Ann, feeling an anxiety that had never possessed him for as long as he could remember. Even with Beth, at the peak of their love, he had never experienced anything like this. It was drunkenness, it was peace and it was ecstasy itself, all rolled up into one emotional lump that choked him violently in soft velvet waves.

He reached for Ann, feeling the softness of her.

She came into his arms, her firm, supple breasts cushioning against him, hot and silken, cushions, full, yielding, breathing and alive with desire and passion.

For a long time neither of them moved, but merely held each other close, as if attempting to absorb some life, some soul, some emotional being from the other. There was magic to the simplicity of merely being close, without going through the motions of passion, without moving and to only be aware of one another in a most intimate way.

The movement of her breasts against his chest created the first sensation of need within him. Then he felt the hardening of nipples stab at him and the desire became

160

stronger.

Ann shifted, her thighs pressed tighter and her lips touched his throat.

That subtle movement was like a spark between them, exploding something so raw and basic that it left him dazed.

They tensed and then all at once her lips were on his and they were kissing. It was a deep, passionate kiss that used every inch of their bodies, every nerve, every muscle.

As the kiss broke he heard Ann's voice sigh, "Oh, Joe...Joe..." And even though no more was said, it seemed to him as if she were revealing an inner emotion of love. She had exposed all her needs, all her being, in those words.

They shifted and then she was on her back, her hands covering his head, her breasts soft, hot, surging up against his kisses.

The passion took over then. It was a basic, animal passion that mixed with the emotional. The physical with the love, moving through them like an electric current, firing, directing their actions beyond their will.

And all the time his mind was screaming over and over again how much he loved her, how he loved her more than he could ever express. Yes with every touch, every kiss, every caress he tried to communicate those feelings to her, desperately attempted to drown her with the loving joy he was brimming over with, the stunning flood of emotion.

I love you. I love every inch of you. I don't care who knows it. I love you, dearest Ann.

Their bodies joined in the final act of love, as their hips glided together. United, he felt the words of love flooding out past his lips, the need controlling his vocal cords, making it impossible to resist their demanding order to speak to her, to tell her how he felt, to let her know the love that possessed him.

"Oh, Ann, Ann, I love you...love you...love you..."

And the words seemed to accent the movement of their bodies and then everything blurred, and sensation was all there was, a wonderful, full and complete sensation of two lovers giving fully, receiving fully all there was to experience in life.

His voice continued to speak the words of love, even after the ecstasy had washed away.

The two of them clung to one another for a long time and he was telling her over and over again that she was everything to him that nothing else mattered in life.

Finally they slipped away from each other and lay side by side.

It was some time before sanity returned, before the drunken passion had completely washed itself away.

Ann turned, looked down at him, her eyes bright. He reached up, caressed her face with his hand, said: "I don't know how you feel, Ann, but...marry me...just marry me and don't think about anything else."

Her eyes softened as they looked into his. She took a deep breath, and her large breasts pressed his arm.

"Joe...I don't know...it's all too fast...and my career and—"

"Forget that. If you want it...later...we'll work out something. But...I love you, Ann. That's all I know and it is all I care about. I don't give a damn about anything else. You've overwhelmed me totally."

He pulled her close, covered her face with kisses, caressed her back and then tensed as he said once more, "Marry me, Ann. Please make my life worth living...say something! Say yes, that you love me, that you want the same thing...oh, crap!"

He knew he'd gone too far and felt like a damned silly jerk. How could she possibly feel the same way? They were almost total strangers.

He waited for her to say something—anything.

But she was silent, saying nothing.

After a while they broke away from the embrace and then Ann sat up, looked at the far wall, thoughtfully.

"I don't know, Joe. I...I know how I feel about you...and I..." She turned and looked at him and there was desperation in her eyes. "Oh, damned, why did this have to happen to me?"

Joe felt sickness grind at him. He sat up, held her shoulders.

"Joe, I don't want to think about it right now. It's all

162

too fast. It just doesn't fit into my plans and I have to get used to the idea and—"

A welling excitement took over Joe's action.

"I can't hope for more," he told her. "After all, we hardly know each other, really...but that doesn't make any difference to me. I know I love you." His eyes pleaded with her to tell him how he stood.

"Joe, I think I feel the same way—but...it's all too...just too fast. Let's wait, see...see what happens!" She smiled, then hugged herself to him.

"Love me, Joe...and let's not think about anything else—nothing else at all, not right now."

Then he was crushing her to him, kissing her face, shoulders and finally lips.

After that the melody of love patterned itself into a concerto of passion without thought, without reason and became strangely beautiful beyond Joe's ability to even understand it.

All he knew was that he had a chance, and that was all he needed.

Joe knew it was necessary to leave Ann Farrow that evening. The business of Carol Clements' had to be taken care of. How he would manage that, Joe had no way of knowing.

It was well past six when he left Ann's apartment and started driving for his own place to change. After having made love to Ann, and having declared his love, it would be impossible to touch another woman. Joe knew that and he realized that it was necessary to find some means to get Carol Clements to understand his position. How he would manage that, Joe didn't have the least idea.

All the way home his mind was spinning with thoughts about Ann, Carol and the future—a future that could be shattered somewhat by Carol if she wanted to.

As he drove up to his apartment and turned off the engine, a sense of depression set in to attack the joy of love that had become so strong and powerful. It was almost as if he guessed that things couldn't go on like this—that something had to happen. What he didn't realize was that it had already happened.

163

Getting out of the car he went to his apartment. As he came to the door he spotted an envelope tacked onto it.

Puzzled, Joe pulled the envelope off and then tore it open.

A typewritten message was on the paper inside.

"Dear Joe. Call me at once, June."

More puzzled, Joe went into the apartment and moved immediately to the phone, dialing June's home phone.

After several rings June's voice said: "Hello?"

"June, Joe."

"Oh, Joe, I've been trying to get hold of you all afternoon. Just a little after you left the office the police arrived, and..."

"What happened?" Joe asked, startled, a pounding throb hit his head like hammers. A grinding sensation touched his stomach. That ulcer was coming, coming too close, he thought automatically.

"It's..." June's voice hesitated, then continued: "It's Beth. She was killed last night...an auto accident. They wanted you to identify her body. Something like that and—"

Joe didn't hear the rest.

His mind said: *It wasn't that he still loved her...but you couldn't completely stop loving a woman you had married and planned so much with...*

Beth was dead. It didn't seem possible. How could she end that way? Why? How'd it happen?

So many questions struck him at one. He just stood there unable to move, hardly able to think.

Joe felt sickness touch his throat. He heard his name being called over and over again and it was some time before he reacted.

"Joe, are you there...are you all right?" June's voice cried over the receiver.

Finally he said: "Yes...yes, I'll be all right...I guess."

Slowly he hung up the phone.

Dazed, shaken, Joe turned, left the apartment, blindly found his car.

CHAPTER SIXTEEN

Ann couldn't sleep. She had been trying for a long time, but her thoughts kept returning to what Joe had told her, what he had offered.

Marriage.

That was madness! Delicious, wonderful, insane crazy madness.

It was all too much to accept. Too fast. It buckled all her plans. Every emotional fiber of her body was fighting against the pleasure that his words had built into a glowing fire within her.

She didn't want him to be in love with her. She didn't want to care about Joe Dickenson or any man. She wanted to use Joe, to get ahead with her career.

But it was happening all too fast, much too fast. Finally she got up from bed, went into the kitchen, found the half-empty bottle of scotch and poured herself a drink.

What in the hell did she want in life, really? That was what he had asked.

Happiness, simply happiness.

But would it be possible to be happy with a man like Joe Dickenson? Could she find a peace of mind with him and a sense of meaning out of her life as his wife?

Damned Joe, she cursed inwardly, taking a swallow of Scotch and starting for the bedroom.

She lay down in bed again, and looked up at the dark ceiling, trying to think of anything other than the tormenting thoughts about the possible future with Joe. Tormenting, exciting, lovely, confusing, crazed visions.

Everybody reached a moment in time, a fork in their life's road where they could move in one direction or another. And everything would be changed. They would never be able to return to the fork.

Hers was simple.

Marry Joe. And let things develop, as they will ... without thought of career one way or the other.

Or use Joe for the purpose of The Career—and possibly happiness, too.

That was the puzzle she had to work out, now. Before it was too late. For once she had made a decision it would be possible to move. Until then, she would stand still.

It was impossible to make any immediate decisions in any case. Even if she did want to marry him, and did so, how would she know for sure why? Was it for love, or for what he could do for her as an Actress, Star?

That would ruin any happiness they might have in any case.

"Why did things have to become so damned complicated?" she asked herself, closing her eyes, trying to blot out the thoughts.

But they continued to haunt her. The dream, which suddenly seemed vague and difficult to focus on, was at best something she had believed possible, something to aim for, to drive all her energies to create. But was it realistic? What Joe had told her about the difficulties of an acting career was obviously realistic. And they haunted her thoughts along with the pleading of his voice asking her to marry him.

She didn't want to think about all that. She wanted to escape all those thoughts.

She fought for sleep, which didn't come easily.

* * * * * * *

Joe was in a bar, somewhere in Hollywood, but only vaguely aware of the location.

A lot had taken place in the last few hours.

Going to the police. Identifying Beth's pitiful and broken body. Hearing the reports that the police had been given.

Beth had walked out across the street, right in front of an on-rushing car. Every witness had thought she had done

166

so on purpose. The police had shrugged helplessly when he had asked if they believed it was suicide. "It's hard to tell; maybe you can give us some information on that."

Joe had purposely declined to give them any information. The less said, the better, he realized.

But it was impossible to turn off his thoughts.

He had refused to make love to Beth. He had bluntly rejected her in total. What more terrible a thing can a man do to a woman? If only he had thought! If only he had realized what could happen—the hurt that Beth had felt.

But no, he had been numb, uncaring. Involved in his own world of problems, and anxious to get rid of her.

Damned Carol Clements. There was a woman he hated with every nerve in him. Hated with the same amount of passion that he loved Ann Farrow.

The world was dim around him, like he was in some kind of dimensionless space, which had no shape, no time, or sound. Only his thoughts kept running, running over and over again in his mind, without shape, screaming out their rambling pattern of confusion.

He couldn't continue with Carol. That was simple enough. He couldn't possibly keep that up, no matter what it cost. It had cost too much already.

Dear little Beth. If only she had understood. If only he had been able to understand her need. If only...But there were too many "if only's," and none of them could really be answered.

Joe looked up, tried to find the bartender, finally spotted the man, motioned and waited.

Another double scotch settled in front of him and he grabbed it with shaky hands.

The liquor hardly burned any more. It seemed like he was drinking water. Nothing seemed to affect him, other than the thoughts running over and over again, saying the same thing like a perverse mantra.

His life was a mess. There was direction, but the price of that direction was far too high. But how could he let go? He was holding a tiger and the danger of letting go of the tail was to be gobbled up.

He thought of Carol, realizing that the woman would

be furious. But she would have to understand that there were other things in a person's life other than Carol Clements and satisfying her sick body.

Yet she was a key to too many elements.

If he had a chance with Ann, in or out of marriage, it might be very important to keep his job, on more than one level. If she wanted to become a successful actor, then he would only be of used to her as a power broker in the film industry. If he lost that he might lose his possible hold on her, his advantage to her.

God, how horrible that thought was. So terribly perverted. Yet damn realistic.

Slowly Joe rose from the stool and moved away from the bar. He staggered toward the entrance and then suddenly he was outside. The cold evening breeze hit his face like a frozen hand.

He thought about Carol Clements and thought about his future—a very questionable one unless he could make Carol realize the truth about himself and about life.

And why he wasn't serving her bod that very moment!

The woman was sick, inside, emotionally, mentally. All sick and mixed up. She didn't realize the time of day and didn't understand the realities of life.

Joe searched the street and saw a gas station at the corner.

There should be a telephone booth there.

Joe moved, swaying with every step, finding it hard to walk a straight course. Finally he came to the gas station and spotted a telephone booth.

Making his way there he tried to remember Carol's number. It was like trying to read through a blurry telephone book, the numbers out of focus and distant.

Finally he stepped into the booth, fished into his pocket, fumbled, and at last managed to pull out a fist full of change.

Some of the money fell to the floor at his feet, but he ignored it.

Picking up the receiver he placed fifteen cents into the phone and then cursed himself and dropped more coins.

168

Then he started dialing, automatically, without trying to remember. The numbers popped into his brain, one at a time. Finally the phone was ringing.

Then a voice said hello, and he asked to speak to Carol Clements, telling the voice who he was.

"You no good bastard, where are you?" the voice cried.

"Something came up, Carol," he announced in a slurred voice, recognizing her for the first time.

"Nothing comes up when I want you! You understand?" The words were cruel and demanding, almost hysterical. The voice of a woman near madness. That was Carol. Get her way or else.

"I can't make it, Carol," Joe said. Then foolishly added: "Ever again!"

There was a long silence and then Carol's voice came threateningly over the phone.

"Joe, you get your ass over here right now, or you are finished. Walter Bennick won't like it when I don't turn up tomorrow. He won't like it at all. And you will be the one who is finished—*not* me!"

Then the receiver went suddenly dead.

For some time Joe stood there. It seemed like a horrid kind of fantasy, a kind of terrible nightmare from which he could not wake. It was incredible that anybody could be so selfish as Carol Clements could. Her logic, or reasoning, was all twisted up. She wanted to continue making pictures, believing that it was possible to continue her little games of playing the Big Star and get away with it.

Maybe she was right.

But maybe not.

Didn't she realize that this picture might just be her last chance?

Or didn't she care?

Joe moved, dropped the receiver and then left the phone booth. It was some moments before he could locate himself and remember where he had parked his car.

Slowly he started down the street, determined to have it out for the last time with Carol. Suddenly he didn't care about anything other than getting the woman off his back—

for good.

Somehow he had to attempt to make her realize that she had more to gain playing ball with the studio than by playing games. She had her career at stake and didn't realize it.

If he could only make her admit it. If only he could force her to see the truth as it really was, his own career would be saved.

This would be a last ditch stand, Joe realized and he wasn't really in any kind of condition to be polite or gentle about it.

And maybe that was the best kind of condition to be in.

Perhaps it was the only way such a woman as CC could be handled realistically. No holds barred, no wiggle room. Just hard damning facts.

CHAPTER SEVENTEEN

Carol was sitting in the living room when the maid ushered Joe in.

She looked up and from the expression in her eyes there was no doubt that a scene of violent emotions was in the offing. Violence of a nature he may never have known before with this woman.

"You may go home," Carol told the maid.

She didn't say anything until the maid had left some ten minutes later.

It was a long awkward silent wait. The darkening quiet before the storm. Both of them seemed to try to ignore each other until they were alone.

Joe smoked several cigarettes and paced. He tried to think of how he would go about battling the next moments. But the sense of awkwardness, the wait, the knowing what was to happen, made his mind merely run around and around in circles. The liquor was still buzzing, but strangely the drive to Carol's home had given him some control over his actions. He felt damned high, but not falling down drunk. There was too much that depended on what happened between the two of them.

Finally the maid went out the front door. Then Carol stood, started toward him.

"Now, Joe, what's the trouble?" she inquired in a controlled voice, stopping some two yards from him.

They stood in the middle of the large living room, glaring at each other like two animals about to make a savage, deadly charge, about to do mortal combat with one another.

Carol's face was drawn tight, her features pinched

171

and hard, her eyes cold, demanding. She stood there in front of him; legs parted about two feet, as if balancing herself for some physical blow. But those eyes burned into his, challenging, demanding an answer when there was none.

"Carol," he finally said, trying to keep his voice calm, "Don't you understand anything about human beings? Don't you—?"

"What the hell does that mean!" she spat out, her lips thin, almost cruel.

"You can't force people to do things they don't want to. You should know that!" Joe announced firmly, beginning to warm up to his statement.

"I wouldn't *think* of forcing anybody to do anything! You are my man, and that's all I know. And you better get to understanding that, right now—and soon."

"Carol—it's finished, done with! We had nothing and could never have anything. You should know that!"

The woman suddenly laughed. It was a taunting, victorious laugh.

"You'll do everything I tell you, Joe Dickerson. You marry me like you promised the other night and you'll be my husband and you won't move, breath or think about anything except when I tell you to." There was a high pitched insanity to her voice.

Joe stood there, then said what his mind was screaming. "What are you talking about?"

"The other night...surely you remember. You won't forget that. I asked you to marry me—and you said you would. You said you would marry me and that's all there is to it. Now, do as I tell you. Get us a drink!" She started to turn, to move toward the sofa.

Joe jerked forward. His hand lashed out to her shoulder, pulled her around to face him.

"I don't know what you have in mind, but you won't get away with anything like that!"

"Like what, Darling?" she cooed, her eyes flashing, very sure of herself.

"Like anything to do with marriage—or *anything* between the two of us! This is finished! Kaput!"

"But you wanted to marry me and I believed you. I'll

172

tell that to a court and they will believe me. They would never believe you!" Carol pointed out. "But that doesn't matter. You see, if you don't do exactly what I tell you—your job and future will be finished—for good! Nobody in Hollywood will touch you and just smoke that up your ass for a while!"

She twisted from his grip. "And don't you ever touch me again, unless I tell you to!"

Joe felt disgusted and a little pity for this woman. She was very beautiful in body, but ugly in mind. If she had a soul it was damaged.

Slowly he turned, started for the front door.

"I just came over to tell you it was finished between us," he announced, facing her at the entranceway.

"You just do that, Joe. But you won't get anywhere! Tomorrow you won't see me at the studio—and I think that will fix your little wagon!" She laughed, then settled down on the sofa. Very sure of herself.

Too sure.

Joe sighed, decided to try once more.

"Go ahead, Carol. Ruin your career. That's all right with me. But before you start doing things that could harm you very much, you better listen to me." He started across the room.

"I don't want to hear!" she announced. "Either fix a drink or walk out! Make up your mind, buddy!"

Joe stopped in front of her, stood there looking down at the beautiful features of Carol Clements, Hollywood Star.

"Carol, if you flub this picture, you *will* be finished. And that's the truth. The only reason Walter hired you was because you would come cheap and make a hit out of a flop property. *Roaring Guns* is a stinker without a star. But...believe me, this was your last chance. It is your only last chance. You're considered poison. Nobody would hire you before and if you flub this people will just laugh at you. Maybe you don't hear the truth; maybe you do, but don't listen. But the truth is that you have been washed up for a very long time. A beautiful, talented actress, washed up because she won't face life and Hollywood in a realistic way. Studios won't put up with your kind of antics. This is a business and

173

run by businessmen and in a business-like manner. They don't care about you. They care about profits. And an actor like you just costs too much! You aren't professional acting. If you don't believe that, it is your own neck. I fought to get you for the part, because I thought it might be good for the studio. I even liked you on the screen and thought it a crime that you were sliding out of focus.

"You take my word for it, Carol. I might be washed up by you not playing it straight, but so will you. And if you have one grain of honesty in your damned brain, you'll know that's true! Make a go at this film and make a hit at the box-office and you will be solid with many offers. *No* star is above the Hollywood money people. You can't buck City Hall or Hollywood producers. Either you get on the ball or you will be finished. Don't believe me if you don't care. You gamble your life away. I don't give a shit any more!"

She started to say something, started to stand, but Joe pushed her back down onto the sofa.

"Shut up and listen, just once in your life. You're a nobody! Just a nobody unless Hollywood and the money decide you are something. Hollywood can take a person—a nobody—and make them into a star if they so desire. Any beautiful body with the ability to speak lines in front of the camera. That's all they need. You'd be surprised how many actors can't act at all without a cutting room making them look good. And that's the lay of the land. Big names made good in a cutting room. That's the beauty of Hollywood and movies. It is all make-believe—and the biggest make-believe is many times the statement that a person can act! You don't need acting talent to get ahead in Hollywood. Just a body, a press agent, a manager, an agent and money to promote you. Right contacts with a body beautiful will make a star. And don't think you have any edge over anybody else just because you know how to act. You act. Fine. A sex-pot. And you're a damned fucking good lay. But—so what? Many women can fuck a guy. And can make all men want to be with them in bed. No secret in that. And you do a good job, when you want to. So...why don't you grow up? Act your age. Stop being a whore. Be a professional actor. Work and work hard. Forget the past, if there's anything in it that has

174

made you the way you are. You just can't get away with playing the game your way. You do that—and you are finished as of this movie. And don't kid yourself. Those are the facts of life. That's what'll make you or break you. You've reached the end of the road and you either make a right turn or you drown in your own shit."

He stood there for a long time, exhausted by his outburst, knowing the complete defeat that was his to now face. Those words had doomed his career.

Carol Clements just wasn't the type of person to believe him.

She couldn't.

And because of that, he was finished.

Sick, Joe left the image of Carol's distorted, face looking up into his with such open hatred. It was drained white, but the rage and confusion in her eyes was obvious. There was no doubt as to what she would do and what she was planning or thinking.

He'd blown his career in one raging explosion. And actually didn't care any more. She was, at last, off his back!

PARLEY IN PASSION, BY CHARLES NUETZEL

CHAPTER EIGHTEEN

How long she had been asleep, Ann didn't know. It seemed only a minute.

The knocking on the door was like the pounding of a steel hammer, and had a desperation that startled her.

Who could it be?

There was only one person who knew where she lived. And that was Joe Dickenson.

A flutter rushed through Ann as she quickly slipped from bed. Without thinking, she moved toward the front door, dressed only in a thin nightgown.

What could Joe want?

She flung open the door and Joe pushed in, his face drawn tight and tragic, his eyes red-rimmed, his mouth sagging.

Slowly closing the door, Ann felt a flood of compassion and something else that ate painfully at her.

"What's wrong?" she breathed.

Joe didn't say anything, but instead pulled her into his arms. For a long time he clung to her like a little boy, lost, desperate. The change in him was startling.

"What's wrong?" she repeated as he slowly moved away from her.

Joe stepped to the overstuffed chair that was opposite the sofa, fell down into it and sat there staring across at the wall.

The little light that came in from the bedroom cast deep shadows across his features.

He looked tired and defeated.

"Joe...want to talk about it?" Ann inquired, moving to his side, feeling a swelling excitement at the fact he was here. Something was desperately wrong and he had come to her.

What could have happened in such a short time? Everything had been so wonderful when he had left. Now, this...

Slowly Joe looked up at her, then lowered his eyes.

"It can't be *that* terrible," she soothed, caressing his cheek. A flood of tenderness took control of Ann and suddenly she wanted to comfort Joe, to hold him close, to heal the obvious wounds, whatever they might be.

"Every...everything is finished," Joe finally breathed. Then suddenly the words flooded out. They came so fast that it was hard to adjust to one idea before another flooded out. First he told her about his ex-wife's death, then about Carol Clements. He held nothing back. His words, voice, were filled with self-disgust.

When he was finished, Joe looked up at her, shook his head, said: "I'm sorry...what do you want with my troubles?"

She stood there, looking down and wondered the same thing. What did she want with his troubles?

It would be so simple. Tell him to leave. Be done with him. He could be of no use to her anymore. He had sold himself to the devil and lost. What good was he to any woman wanting a career? What good to any woman, in any case? Period. A defeated man. No future.

Slowly Joe stood, starting towards the door. "Thanks, Ann. You don't know how...nice it was talking to you. I needed to talk to somebody." He hesitated at the door, then turned, facing her. "Thanks for everything, Ann. If things had only been different...if so many things had been different. But..."

He shrugged, then started to open the door.

Ann felt her heart fluttering. Tightness settled over her, a hard lump constricted her throat.

Let him go, her mind screamed, as she started forward. *Let him go! He can't be of any use to you, now.*

But already she was at his side.

Then suddenly she threw her arms around him.

"Oh, Joe...Joe...I love you...that's all I care about ...and there isn't anything else of importance. I don't know

178

why or how. But it happened. Maybe now...maybe now I'm not afraid to admit it. Now that...that things *have* changed."

Then suddenly they were kissing, tenderly and finally passionately. And totally lost in their fantasy with and about one another. Their reality was starting and they dove into it without thought of the future. Only the moment counted and that was in each other's arms.

* * * * * * *

It was eleven that evening when Joe and Ann stepped into his apartment. There were a few things he had to get before they left for Las Vegas. It had happened so fast that he really wasn't even sure of his motives any more. It seemed to him that he was taking so much, and giving so little. But as Ann had said, they would have each other and the future would take care of itself.

Joe told Ann to fix them some drinks while he started to pack.

As he pulled out his suitcase from the closet, the phone suddenly rang.

For a moment he almost ignored it. Then slowly he moved to the hallway, where the phone hung on the wall.

Picking up the receiver, Joe said. "Hello?"

It was Mari Thornton who said: "Oh, Joe, what happened? I tried to get you...all evening. You were supposed to have a date with me at lunch!"

The voice was silent for a long moment, waiting for his reply.

The luncheon date seemed far away, as did everything. Reality was far away.

Finally he said: "Sorry, things came up."

"How about tomorrow? It's important." Her voice was harsh.

"Forget it...I won't be in town."

"Where are you going?" Mari cried, alarmed.

"Las Vegas for a fast marriage," he announced, firmly, wanting to be rid of Mari.

"Marriage?" Mari fairly shouted into the receiver. "Who in the world with?"

"Ann...Ann Farrow!"

There was a split second silent reply, then Mari cried: "Are you kidding? Listen Joe...you don't want to marry her. That lesbian bitch."

The word hit Joe like a slap. For a moment he stood there, dazed.

"What the hell are you talking about!" Joe snapped, numb.

"That's what I wanted to see you about. Ann tried to love me up. She did a lot of dirty things...I *kicked* her out!" Mari's voice was tight with victory. There was just an edge to the tone she used as to startle Joe.

Slowly, without saying another word, Joe hung up, stared at the phone. His mind was racing, fighting through a series of arguments.

Finally he turned, stepped into the living room, looked at Ann, who was sitting on the sofa, her legs up under her, the skirt over her knees.

She smiled, just a light, warm smile.

A Lesbian? His mind chanted. *But how? How?* It didn't seem possible. No woman who gave of herself like that could be a Lesbian. Ann was too passionate.

No woman could be that passionate and not mean it. Unless she was a fantastic actress. And with what motive after what had happened to him yesterday? He was not used to a woman wanting to fool him as a career move. He was useless in that way.

A Lesbian might be cold like Mari, like a prostitute, going through actions.

They certainly wouldn't want to marry a man like him, without any future. If he still had a future at *Bennick Studios*...

"Who was that?" Ann inquired casually.

For a moment only Joe hesitated.

His mind asked: *If Ann was a Lesbian, then why would she want to marry him? It wouldn't make sense. No, there could only be one explanation to Mari's call. Mari surely must have reversed the roles. It was the only logical explanation.*

"Who was it?" Ann repeated pleasantly.

"Oh, nobody," Joe laughed. "Just some girl...I used to know. I believe she's a Lesbian."

He turned, went into the bedroom and then packed.

EPILOGUE

The only thing that had marred the honeymoon was the realization that there was nothing to go back to. Yet, in a strange way, it didn't seem to affect their happiness. They were like two kids on a holiday. Two wonderful weeks in the city of glamour and seeing very little of the gambling tables, very little of what Las Vegas had to offer. But they had everything in each other's arms.

But it was when they returned to Hollywood that they had to face the facts of life.

Joe felt an icy feeling of defeat as he drove into the Bennick Studio parking lot. He had to face the downfall. There were too many personal items, too many loose ends that simply had to be tied up before he could be completely free of the Studio.

After parking his car, Joe walked across the street, toward the Studio entrance.

As he approached the guard on duty the man grinned, said: "Good-morning, Mr. Dickenson."

"Hello. How's the kids, Tom?" Joe asked, feeling a little warmth.

At least everybody didn't know about his humiliating defeat.

"Fine."

"I have to go in and get some things taken care of," Joe said, almost as if he expected the guard to not allow him in.

"Of course. The Boss has been going out of his mind trying to get hold of you." The guard grinned again. "Where you been?"

"In Vegas, getting married."

"You're kidding!"

"Not in the least. Something good has to come out of this nightmare!" He forced a laugh.

"Well, welcome to the club!" the man said, warmly extending his hand.

As Joe left the guard he felt a strange sense of happiness that didn't really make sense. Maybe the future wasn't as bad as it seemed. Maybe Ann had been right. After all, they had each other and they could start anew, facing the next days—years—together, come what may, for better or for worse, till death did them in!

Several people greeted him as he passed them.

He wondered if June would be there. Probably. She went with the office. Maybe they had already moved his things out.

He was just entering the office building when he suddenly bumped into June rushing towards him.

Her face was bright as she exclaimed: "The gate guard phoned me you were here! Joe, you wonderful old dog, going up and getting married like that. You should have told us!"

She threw her arms about his neck, hugging him. "It's wonderful..." Then she frowned. "A lot of girls are going to be very unhappy."

"Thanks," he said awkwardly. June was that kind of woman. She would look at the bright side of things.

"I came to collect some of my things," he told her, starting for his office.

June hesitated, took his arm, said: "Mr. Bennick wants to see you, Joe."

"To hell with him."

"Come on, do as mother-June tells you." She looked at him with a strange look in her eyes.

"What's going on?" Joe asked. "Surely he can wait to cut me down to size! Slice my throat!"

June's face was blank as she forced him along the hall toward Bennick's office.

In silence he followed.

As they entered the outer office, the secretary looked up, nodded toward the inner office. "He's expecting you."

June followed as they went into the studio head's office.

"Close the door," Bennick growled from behind his desk, his face stern, his eyes shadowed.

June closed the door behind him.

Walter Bennick slowly stood.

"Well, do you want to explain yourself?" he demanded in a harsh voice. A little too harsh.

"What's there to explain?" Joe countered, wishing he could turn and walk out. There really wasn't anything keeping him. This man didn't really have any power over him any more. On the other hand, there was a large check that was due and he had to play along. Let the old man have his fun.

"There's a lot to explain. You walked out, without a word! Explain!"

"I got married."

"That has nothing to do with it." Bennick grinned, a twisted grin of satisfaction. "I've wanted to do this for a long time, Dickenson. As of the moment you left, you were fired! You understand?"

"I understood that before you even knew it would happen," Joe said, starting to turn. "Now that you are through firing me, I think I'll just run along. I have a wife to support."

"You won't get a job at any other studio if I have anything to say about it!" Bennick announced.

June piped in, saying: "Oh, come on, don't be so damned cruel!"

She winked at Joe.

Joe hesitated, stared at June, puzzled.

"That woman," Bennick's voice boomed, "That CC really blew the whistle on you and everything alive within hearing distance!"

"Let's cut the cat and mouse, Walter!" Joe snapped, looking at the studio head. "You've had your fun. Now let me get the hell out of here!"

Bennick shouted: "Shut up!"

There was such violent emotion in his voice that Joe was stunned to silence.

185

Slowly Bennick continued. "I have a lot more to say. I've just begun. Now you just sit down and listen to me!"

June's hands pushed Joe forward. Like a zombie he was shoved into a chair facing Bennick's desk.

The big man settled in the chair behind the desk and leaned over toward Joe.

"Now, I don't know what you said to CC, but you said one hell of a lot, no doubt. I don't care to know. It doesn't make any difference, now."

"Look, that's in the past is finished. Now please—"

"Shut up and listen!" Walter Bennick said in a soft whisper. "You are just about the most impossible fellow I've ever met!"

He was silent for a moment, then continued: "Since you were away, getting married and all that romantic crap, you couldn't know what actually happened here."

"I can guess."

"Be quiet and listen." Bennick took a cigar out of a box on the desk in front of him, then after lighting it, said: "CC, Big Star, Hollywood trouble-maker, Motion Picture problem child suddenly made a turn about. Ever since you have been gone, Carol came to the Studio every day, each and *every* day. She was a professional. She signed a contract to do one picture a year with us for the next five years, when she finished *Roaring Guns.*"

Joe felt like he had been slapped across the face. He felt as if the blood had washed out of him.

"So rub it in! She wins, I lose. That's the name of the game!"

"As for you...she had a lot of violent things to say— at first. But..." Bennick grinned, then added, "In the end she changed about that, too."

Joe still sat there, not moving a muscle, trying to figure out what the hell was going on.

"Further more," Bennick continued, "She had you in mind when signing her contract."

"I just bet!" Joe laughed sarcastically. "I can imagine!"

"You would lose that bet, Joe," Bennick announced pleasantly. "If it weren't for her I would have taken at least

186

some kind of action against you...but you deserved a vacation anyway. And there isn't anything much for you to do for another couple of weeks, anyway."

'What the hell are you talking about?" Joe managed, for the first time almost praying that what seemed to be true just might be true.

"She said no contract unless Joe Dickenson was made her personal producer on each movie!" Bennick grinned. He pulled out a cigar from the box on the desk, extended it toward Joe.

"Have one, big producer!"

ABOUT THE AUTHOR

Charles Nuetzel was born in San Francisco in 1934, and writes:

"As long as I can remember I wanted to be a writer. It was a dream I never thought would materialize. But with the help of Forrest J Ackerman, who became my agent, I managed to finally make it into print.

"I was lucky enough not only in selling my work to publishers but also ending up packaging books for some of them, and finally becoming a 'publisher' much like those who had bought my first novels. From there it as a simple leap to editing not only a sci-fi anthology, but a line of sci-fi books for Powell Sci-Fi back in the 1960s. Throughout these active professional years I had the chance to design some covers and do graphic cover layouts for pocket books & magazines."

Much of his work in covers and graphics are a result of having had a father who was a professional commercial artist, and who did a number of covers for sci-fi magazines in the 1950s and later for pocket books—even for some of Mr. Nuetzel's books.

In retirement he has become involved in swing dancing, a long time lover of Big Band jazz. But more interestingly world travels have taken him (and his wife Brigitte) across the world, to Hawaii, Caribbean, Mexico, Kenya, Egypt, Peru, having a life-long interest in ancient civilizations. His website is full of thousands of pictures taken during these trips.

www.ingramcontent.com/pod-product-compliance
Lightning Source LLC
Chambersburg PA
CBHW020610250626
47154CB00004B/1450